T

Thorn
Farm

Denise Clarke

Top Thorn Farm

Editing and formatting by Amanda:

www.letsgetbooked.com

AUTHOR'S NOTE

When I was a librarian in a rural secondary school, students were expected to read a fiction book during their weekly library lesson, and I would sometimes be approached by frustrated students complaining there was nothing on the shelves to interest them. Even when I guided them towards popular fantasy and adventure stories, they sadly shook their heads, so I asked them what their interests were. The answer was often, 'Farming stuff, driving tractors and bikes.' These young people alerted me to a substantial gap in the market. I hope that they will enjoy this story.

CHAPTER 1

Jamie Bouthwaite spilled out of the minibus as it lurched to a halt in the narrow lane beside a farm entrance and cattle grid. He was the last of the ten Mereside Academy students to be dropped off.

'Thanks. See yer lay'er,' Jamie muttered to the driver, as he stuffed his phone into a sagging blazer pocket and slammed the bus door shut.

Hoisting his rucksack onto his back, he turned towards the stony track and began the mile and a half trek to Top Thorn Farm. At fifteen, he was a tall, well-built boy and often sprinted it with ease. But today, his rucksack was well stuffed and sat awkwardly on his back, causing him to adjust it several times for comfort, so he walked. As well as bulky coursework files, he was carrying his rugby kit, made filthy from the muddy pitch. Mum would grumble at the state of it, but she'd cheerfully wash it all, ready for next week.

It had been drizzling all day and still the clouds hung low, obscuring the breath-taking view of Cumbrian fells, now turned rusty gold by the onset of late autumn. The solitariness that he loved closed in around him, the only sounds being the bleating of sheep and the occasional cry of a lone crow. Kicking a loose rock along the track with his scuffed shoes, he thought reluctantly about the homework that needed doing for the next day. A bit of geography. Not too hard. He could manage that all right. *What about English?* He pushed a hand under the heavy fringe of sandy hair that fell over his freckled brow. What was that essay question they'd been set?

Compare and contrast the characters of Tybalt … (and some other guy?) in Shakespeare's Romeo and Juliet.

He'd had a week to do it and still hadn't even started! Unless he could somehow perform a miracle tonight, Mrs Wilson would give him yet another detention. That woman always knew if you'd copied and pasted stuff you'd found by googling.

He swore softly to himself. It was times like this that he missed his sister Sally, because she had done this GCSE work herself fairly recently and could give him some handy pointers. In the past, she hadn't been above a bit of bribery, like taking on one of her chores. The thought of texting or emailing her now crossed his mind, but he dismissed it as a non-goer. She was in her first term at university now and wouldn't want to be bothered. He certainly wouldn't if he was in her shoes!

Plop! The rock he'd been kicking landed in a puddle that had collected in a deep pothole. One thing was for sure, he would *not* be going to university. Nor would anyone persuade him to stay on at school for sixth form. He wasn't academically inclined and longed to chuck away anything to do with schoolwork as soon as possible and take up farming full time. In his mind's eye, he saw himself on the quad bike bucketing across the fields and heather tracks checking and moving sheep, working dawn 'til dusk at lambing time, cropping grass for silage in summer and then later at the County Show, standing proudly with his prize-winning tups.

Frustratingly, his parents stood in his way. They suggested he should go on to college to get himself some qualification for a trade. *But, what?* Other than farming, little else interested him.

Jamie passed through the second gate along the track, his ears customarily tuned for the rumble of the quad bike or a tractor belonging to Top Thorn Farm. Apart from the occasional hoarse bleats from sheep grazing these acres and the harsh 'kraa kraa' of a crow, there was silence. The drizzle was starting again as the familiar range of stone and concrete outbuildings with their variety of slate and corrugated roofs loomed up. He didn't care about getting wet, he was used to it.

At this time in the afternoon, when he was a little kid, the cows would be making their ponderous way through the bottom meadow and onto the track that led behind the buildings and gave access to the milking parlour. Even now he recalled their mooing to each other, the heavy thud of hooves, the quad bike revving and his father whistling to the dogs. Today Top Thorn, like hundreds of other small farms, no longer had a dairy herd. It didn't pay. The Bouthwaites kept just fifty beef cattle and concentrated chiefly on sheep farming.

Coming into the farmyard, he immediately noticed that the Discovery wasn't parked in its usual place, and then remembered his mother saying at breakfast, she was driving to Carlisle to see the accountant. The house was locked when he pushed his hand down on the door handle, so he used his own key to let himself into the kitchen, made cosy by the warmth of the Aga. He began his ritual of raiding the pantry shelves for whatever treats might lurk there. Then he opened the fridge and helped himself to a banana milkshake. Whilst sitting at the scrubbed pine table with his snack he read the note his mother had left: *'Hotpot in oven. Turn up the heat at 4.30. Back by 6.'*

He went up to his bedroom and swapped his school uniform for jeans and T-shirt. In contrast to the rest of the house, it was a chaotic room with his stuff everywhere. Somewhere, in the midst of it, was an overdue school library book titled *A History of Tractors*. He'd had it out since the end of year 9 and Mr Black, the librarian was coming to the end of his tether over the matter, having sent numerous messages to his form tutor. There was a loan stop on his borrowing account, but there was nothing he wanted to borrow anyway. Perhaps after supper he'd make an effort to look for it, but now, he had more important things to do. Jamie hit the switch on the old PC that he kept solely for gaming and half an hour passed whilst he played.

Suddenly, he remembered his mother's instruction about the hotpot and ran down to the kitchen. He wondered where his father was working. The fact the house had been locked up meant he wasn't close by. There was always plenty to do on a farm, as Jamie knew only too well, but his father was a creature of habit and would usually come into the house for his mug of tea when Jamie arrived off the school bus. Any minute now, his tractor or bike would rumble into the yard.

One of Jamie's chores was feeding the dogs, so he decided to get it done now. His father normally fed the calves at the same time. He stepped into his wellies, grabbed an old jacket that hung behind the door, and went out to the barn across the yard. This was where the dogs lived when they weren't working. Toby, the elder of the two collies, came bounding over on his chain, wagging his brown and white tail in pleasure. 'Good lad!' said Jamie, rubbing the back of the dog's neck. 'Where's Ben, eh?'

He filled up the food bowls with kibble and put one of them down on the floor for Toby. The other dog, he guessed, must be with his father. He stood there for the few minutes it took Toby to devour the food and then let him off the chain to get a bit of exercise outside. To his surprise, the old collie shot off around the side of the buildings and began barking.

Jamie followed; he looked up the track that snaked past the farm buildings and the damson orchard and saw Ben running down to meet him. This struck him as a little unusual. The black and white collie, younger of the farm dogs, always rode with his master, either in the Land Rover, the tractor or on the back of the quad bike. Well trained and highly intelligent, Ben was a loyal worker. He was attuned to Martin Bouthwaite's every command, sometimes responding to just the turn of his head. It was like the dog was hefted to him. 'Ready for your dinner, lad?' Jamie ruffled the thick white ruff of fur around the dog's neck. 'C'mon, then.'

Ben padded slowly after him, but when they reached the barn, he stopped dead, even though his food waited within. 'Don't be daft. Go get dinner!' Still, the dog refused to go into the barn. Jamie repeated his command and when Ben remained outside the barn, his ears cocked up and staring up at him, Jamie frowned in exasperation. 'Oh, well…' he muttered, turned on his heel, and strode off towards the house.

He was flicking through the TV channels when he heard the dogs scratching at the kitchen door and whining. He threw open the door and stuck his head out of the porch. Still no sign of his father. Once again, he pushed his feet into wellies and strolled over the yard to the tractor shed. The green Land Rover was in there along with the John Deere tractor and the quad bike. His father was obviously out in the Massey Ferguson.

Meanwhile, the dogs had followed him, and Ben seemed to be going crazy, moving round in circles and then every so often stopping to stare intently at Jamie. Toby kept giving little barks. It suddenly dawned on

Jamie that the dogs were trying to communicate something to him. How slow he'd been! Something was very wrong. There was no way Ben would have taken off on his own to come home without his master. The dog was far too disciplined. Maybe his master had sent him. Why hadn't Jamie grasped this straightaway?

'Favver!' Jamie said aloud and rushed into the house to call his father's mobile. It didn't ring, but he wasn't surprised to find it was out of signal range. There were only a few spots in this terrain where you could find a signal.

He returned to the dogs and bent down in front of Ben, engaging the collie's gold circled dark eyes that gleamed with intelligence. If only he could speak…

His father's words came back to him. 'Never underestimate a dog. They know more than you think.'

'Let's go find Favver,' he shouted. The dogs immediately understood and wagged their tails.

CHAPTER 2

Jamie rushed back into the porch, took the quad bike's keys from the hook and checked that he had his phone in his pocket before running back to the tractor shed. Within a few moments, he had the bike fired up and was roaring out of the yard towards the track with the dogs sitting in the small bucket trailer fixed behind it. The track was rocky; dry-stone walls, thorny bush and bramble bordered each side. He was used to driving the quad bike on the farm's land and tracks, but obviously kept off the open roads.

Higher and higher, he climbed until the track, which would eventually lead onto Tinder Fell, levelled off by an open field gate. Immediately, Jamie saw the huge shape of the Massey Ferguson tractor with its trailer backed into the entrance of the small barn that was used to store hay bales. Of course, his father would be in there, getting a few bales for the sheep. He heaved a sigh of relief. Perhaps there was nothing wrong after all.

'Eh Favver!' Jamie shouted as he shut down the quad bike and jumped off it. Disciplined to obedience, the dogs stayed where they were in the bucket trailer. All was quiet, and he shouted again before going into the building. He heard a groan from the barn's dim interior and a moment later was shocked to find his father lying on the floor with two heavy oblong bales of hay lying across his legs. These were the big bales, bought in to supplement their own smaller bales that could be handled manually.

'Can't move. Bloody bales came down. Happened so fast … must've disturbed 'em. Can yer get 'em off me, lad?' Martin Bouthwaite inhaled a breath, steeling himself against the excruciating pain and tried to get into a sitting position, but flopped back, groaning.

Instinctively, Jamie dropped to his knees beside his father. 'Dog told me summat were wrong.'

'Stop yer dithering, lad! Pull 'em off me.' Martin let out another painful grunt.

Jamie took a deep breath and pushed at the massive

weights. Bits of hay pricked and tickled his wrists as he worked. *Whew!* Eventually, he freed his father's legs from the restraining bales. He was stronger than most boys of his age, but even so, the effort left him panting and sweating, as he sat back to recover. It was then that he looked up and high above, at the top of the stack. Another bale was partially dislodged, and he realised it could fall at any moment. 'Let's get the hell out of here!' he said.

'Can't move me legs,' his father grunted, struggling unsuccessfully to raise himself. 'P ... Pain's bad.'

'Happen I'll have to pull yer clear. I don't trust them other bales up there are all safe, now that they've been disturbed.' Jamie squatted and placed his hands beneath his father's armpits and tried to move him. Although Martin Bouthwaite didn't carry any surplus fat, he was heavily muscled through manual work, and at first attempt it was impossible to move him single-handed. Jamie knew they needed help, but there was no chance of finding anyone quickly in this desolate spot.

'Can yer help yersel' at all?' he asked breathlessly.

His father raised himself onto his elbows, took a deep breath and heaved, moving his body a few inches before flopping down again. This success instilled a burst of energy in both of them; Jamie put his hands under his father's armpits and pulled him a few more inches. They repeated these actions several times until sufficient space was gained away from the danger area. Both were sweating profusely. They were now close to the trailer at the entrance.

'I'll call an ambulance now.' Jamie groped in his jacket pocket for his phone, switched it on and checked the battery. It still had plenty of charge, but as he suspected, there was no network coverage.

Tha'll have t' gan up yon howe ower there … ter … get … signal,' his father gasped and then gave a yelp of pain, followed by a string of muttered curses.

Jamie stuffed the phone back into his pocket and went outside. The drizzle had now ebbed. He sprinted from the barn and made his way to where the ground rose higher and provided a panoramic view of the farmland that his family owned. In the distance, he could see the house and the range of buildings around the yard.

His father was right about the phone signal. He dialled 999 and waited for the response. It came quickly. A female voice asked which service he required. 'Ambulance,' he said, 'It's me favver. He's been knocked down by some falling hay bales and he can't move his legs and he's in a lot of pain. Might be broken.' As he started to give the location, the thought struck him that an ordinary ambulance might have difficulty accessing the terrain. When he explained this to the emergency call operator, she explained that an appropriate ambulance would be sent.

With the important call made, he phoned the farmhouse, hoping his mother would now be home, but no one picked up. He tried her mobile, and that was switched off. Of course, she must be driving, so he called the landline again and left her a message. He explained what had happened and said that he would wait with his father until the ambulance arrived. Then he walked back down the field to the hay barn. The light was beginning to fade. Glancing at the phone again, he saw it was half-past five. How long would the ambulance take to arrive?

He sat down next to where his father lay propped

against a bale on the barn floor, close to the doorway. 'A shoulda known better,' Martin lamented. There was hay clinging to his thick, brown, slightly greying hair. 'Yer muvver'll kill me fer being so stupid.'

Half an hour passed, and Jamie decided to take the phone up to the point where he could access a signal. As he'd hoped, his mother had arrived home and had tried to call them ten minutes ago. He now called her back. She sounded very calm. 'Jamie, thank goodness you went to look for your father, and well done for calling 999. I'm very proud of you.' Whilst they were talking, she suddenly cried out, 'It's coming now. The ambulance! I'll go out and direct them.'

He ran down the hill and told his father that the ambulance was on its way. 'It's at the farm now. Mum's just seen it. Should be here in a few minutes.' Then he thought about the tractor; it would block the way into the hay barn. He'd better drive it forward a bit.

'Alreet. Keys are in it. Be careful.' His father gave a groan as he attempted to shift position and ease his extreme discomfort.

Jamie climbed up into the cab and started up the big

tractor. Like many farmers' sons, he knew how to drive tractors, despite being too young for a licence. He released the handbrake, selected drive on the automatic gearbox and slowly drove it forward until the trailer was clear of the barn's double doors.

Headlights swept through the gateway and the ambulance stopped, unable to gain better access into the field because Jamie had parked the quad bike in the gateway. He rushed to move it. The dogs, who had sat obediently still all this time, started barking, and he had to quieten them whilst two paramedics jumped out of the ambulance, carrying what looked like a folded stretcher and other bits of equipment. Barely glancing at Jamie, the men headed straight into the barn. He heard them talking to his father. Jamie remained outside; behind him, the vehicle flashed bright lights on and off, and he heard crackling voices and bleeps resounding from its radio.

Soon, the paramedics had Martin strapped onto a stretcher and were lifting him into their ambulance. With high ground clearance and big bumpers, it resembled a jeep; Jamie had seen this type of ambulance used by the Mountain Rescue Service. It seemed a long time before it moved off, as a big fuss was made about securely strapping the stretcher and talking on the radio, presumably to the hospital. Jamie stood at the open door of the vehicle, trying to hear where his father would be taken.

At last, one of the paramedics came to him and said they were going to Lancaster. 'Will me favver…be alreet?' he asked with a slight tremor in his voice.

The man looked at Jamie with concern and asked his age, and if he would be OK. Jamie lied, saying he was sixteen because he knew that his height could pass him as such. 'I'll be reet. I'll just lock up t' tractor and barn, then I'll take bike back down t' farm.'

Doors slammed, the engine started up and the ambulance jeep began its way down the track. Left alone, Jamie was aware of the darkness closing in around him and locked the tractor. He pocketed his father's phone after finding it on the dashboard, and shivered with an unfamiliar sense of sadness and loss. No doubt, his father would be frustrated at not having his phone with him, and he wished that he'd spotted it before the ambulance had left. His eyes began to fill up, and he swallowed. *Yer not a soft cry babby!*

Probably his mother would drive the tractor down to the yard tomorrow. Finally, he secured the barn doors before starting up the bike and turning on its headlights. 'Let's ga'an,' he said to the dogs.

As soon as he arrived in the farmyard, his mother came outside to meet him. He must have looked shaken because she put an arm around him when he dismounted the quad bike. 'How are you, Jamie?'

'I'm reet,' he said quickly. 'But Favver was in a lot of pain.'

'He would be,' she agreed, and her voice wobbled slightly as she gave him a hug. 'They'll give him something to relieve it, don't worry. I just saw him for a few moments when the ambulance came down.' Together, they put the dogs in their kennel and went into the house.

The kettle on the Aga hob was quickly brought up to the boil and Beth Bouthwaite poured two mugs of tea. 'We'll phone the hospital in a couple of hours. Some news should be available by then,' she said.

'Two hours? That's a long time. We could just set off to Lancaster now.' Jamie paced the kitchen impatiently.

'We'd only be hanging about waiting. It'll be better to phone,' she maintained.

'OK.' Jamie's shoulders slumped, and he dropped into a chair. After he'd drunk the tea, he went outside to feed the calves and the two cats that lurked around the buildings, keeping vermin at bay. He checked the cows housed for winter in the largest building. This used to be the milking parlour and was now divided in two sections. They had been mucked out and fed that morning and wouldn't need further attention until tomorrow.

When he returned to the house, his mother, still in the smart skirt and jumper she'd worn for her visit to Carlisle, was plating up the hotpot. He hadn't really felt hungry until the rich aroma of lamb and vegetables met his nostrils, and so he sat down to enjoy it. Then he noticed his mother had only given herself a small portion and was eating slowly, as if deep in thought. He knew she was concerned about his father, but suspected she was also worried about how they would work the farm whilst he was out of action. He was worrying about that himself.

Beth Bouthwaite, like her husband, had farming in

her blood, having been raised on Cumbrian soil. After training as a teacher, she'd returned to her roots to take up her first post in a village primary school, after which she had met and married a farmer. When running the farm consumed their lives, she put her own career on hold. Strong and capable, she could work as hard as a man outdoors, yet keep a neat house and cook hearty family meals.

Whilst she washed up and tidied the kitchen after supper, Jamie texted his friend Josh, and told him briefly about his father's accident. Within a quarter of an hour, the landline phone rang—it was Josh's father. Jamie listened to his mother's side of the conversation. 'Yes, Len … If it hadn't been for Jamie … Yes, it's a bit of a disaster for us … No … No … I'm not sure how we're going to manage whilst Martin's out of action … could be quite a while, but you know what a tough case he is and he'll want to be outside before he should … I'm going to phone the hospital soon and find out what's going on … No … Oh, that's really kind…Yes, day after tomorrow would be great if Neil's free…Great! And if Neil has any regular spare slots in his work schedule, we'll pay him, of course.

I'd really appreciate the help. Thank you *so much,* Len.' She replaced the phone in its charge unit.

The Atkinsons farmed a couple of miles away at Under Clough, the land that bordered Top Thorn, and the two families were great friends. Although the Atkinsons kept some rare breed sheep and cattle, they had diverted into poultry in a very big way.

'I can finish school right now,' suggested Jamie, hoping his father's accident might provide him with an opportunity to get out of having to attend school. But, in his heart, he knew it was unlikely.

'Certainly not! At fifteen, you wouldn't be allowed to, anyway.'

Beth picked up the phone and called the Accident & Emergency Unit at Lancaster. After a few minutes' wait, she was put through to the orthopaedic ward and was told that her husband had sustained two leg fractures and a damaged kneecap. He would need surgery and plaster casts. She related this information to Jamie.

'They told me to call again later tomorrow morning,' she said. 'And now, have you any homework?'

'What?' he gasped in surprise. 'Surely I won't be going ter school tomorrow.'

'Oh yes, you will!' She flicked a lock of blonde hair behind one ear, picked up the mail from the dresser, and marched out of the kitchen.

CHAPTER 3

At half-past five the following morning, Jamie crept downstairs, so as not to disturb his mother, and once he was in the porch, he stepped into farm overalls and wellies. He switched on the power to bring light into the yard and buildings. Next, he strode across the yard to start mucking out the cows. Moving down the aisle between their rows of stalls, he shovelled out piles of fouled straw. There was a machine they used to drag it all outside, and he fired this into action to make a stinking pile in the yard. They would eventually dump it in the midden heap. His next job was to spread fresh straw at the end of each cow stall. They could be fed later. After nearly two hours, he returned to the house.

Tight-lipped, his mother sent him quickly upstairs to shower and get into his school uniform. With breakfast toast in one hand and drinking from a flask of tea held in the other hand, he sat in the Land Rover as she drove him over the bumpy farm track to meet the school bus. He thought she should have been grateful to him for making a good start on the morning's chores, but she didn't seem that way inclined. In fact, she gave him a real dressing down on health and safety. 'You could have had an accident in the cow barn. Using that machine! You could have slipped! Anything could have happened.'

'I'm not a little kid. I've done this job before,' he answered, heaving an exaggerated sigh of impatience.

'Yes, when one of us has been around.'

Josh Atkinson and Nick Dixon were the only boys whom he told about his morning's mucking out, as most of the others in his form wouldn't really be interested or would wrinkle their noses in disgust. 'You can't do it every morning though,' Josh said, casting a look of concern at his friend as they walked down the maths corridor for period 1. They had been best mates all their lives, as had their fathers. Josh was a handsome, confident looking boy who favoured the same shaved back and sides haircut, with longer top as worn by Jamie and most of the others. The brown curls flopping over Josh's brow contrasted with Jamie's straight, fair fringe.

'I can if I go to bed early enough.'

'Rather you than me,' said Nick, trying to catch up with the long strides of the other two. He was short and bespectacled.

'Me brother'll help out. Yer mam won't be stuck on her own wi' it all.' Josh caught the classroom door from the girl in front of them and flashed a smile at her.

Jamie ran into trouble during his last period, when Mrs Wilson reprimanded him for not handing in that English essay on Romeo and Juliet. He wasn't the only one who found it difficult to relate to a Shakespearean tragedy about ill-starred lovers. Nick and a plump, mouthy girl named Becca Ellis were also in trouble. 'Detention for you three!' she declared, 'unless your essays are handed in at the staff room or emailed to me by 8.30 a.m. tomorrow morning.'

When the bus dropped him off that afternoon, Jamie practically ran all the way along the Top Thorn Farm track and burst into the kitchen, throwing down his bag. Beth, in an old pair of jeans and sweatshirt, pushed a mug of tea and a flapjack in front of him.

'Your father's had an operation on his knee this afternoon,' she told him. 'They're bringing him home by ambulance tomorrow morning.'

'Oh, can't you fetch him in t' car?' he asked in surprise.

''Fraid not. He's got plaster casts on both legs.'

Jamie's eyes widened. 'How will he walk? Get t' bog and stuff?'

'I'm sure he'll have crutches and possibly a wheelchair. But he *will* need a bed downstairs for a bit. You can help me with that later.'

Following the farm chores and the evening meal, Jamie and his mother carried the spare single bed frame and mattress down into the sitting room. 'How he'll take to being down here is anybody's guess,' she grimly observed.

They had arranged for Josh's brother Neil, who worked as a contractor on several farms, to come five mornings a week. 'I could have done that.' Jamie's protest was only mild, because although taking on the chore would have made him feel important, he regarded Neil with something close to hero worship.

'Your schoolwork must take priority. I'm not having any more argument on the matter,' retorted his mother. He went to bed with his head full of the farm and didn't remember the English essay until he was walking up the track the next morning to catch the bus.

Consequently, he spent the entire lunch break in the English department with a collection of resources on Romeo and Juliet, from which he managed to pull together an essay that compared and contrasted certain male characters. It seemed like a waste of time to him. In his opinion, it was just words that meant nothing to him, or anyone else, for that matter. He tried to imagine what was happening at the farm and how he could have been usefully occupied.

During period 5, he wondered if his father had already separated the tups. The job needed to be done by the end of the week. With an effort, he dragged his mind back to chemistry.

When he got in from school that afternoon, he found his father in the living room, sitting in a wheelchair. He wore a pair of baggy shorts and both legs in plaster casts were propped on a stool. 'God knows how long I'll be stuck like this,' he said with a scowl on his face. He accepted the mug of tea that Beth brought him without a word of thanks and didn't ask Jamie what kind of day he'd had at school.

'He's cross with himself, not us, though it makes little difference at the moment,' Beth told Jamie in the kitchen. 'He'll settle in a day or two.'

'I s'pose I'd feel the same. Frustrated as hell,' said Jamie.

'And he won't be able to have a smoke.' Beth gave a gleeful laugh.

'Because yer don't allow him to smoke in t' house!' Jamie laughed as well. He knew his father rationed himself to around four cigarettes a day, considering them his little treat. It wouldn't be Jamie's treat! When he was thirteen, out of curiosity, he had stolen one of his father's cigarettes and attempted to smoke it behind the barn. He'd ended up coughing in disgust.

He went outside and did his chores, feeding the calves first, then the dogs and finally the cats. It was a clear, bright evening, with the scents of late autumn and impending winter in the air. He lingered out there for a little while, checking his phone for Snapchat messages from mates.

After the family had eaten supper together on trays in front of the fire, his mother switched off the TV, just as his father was about to catch up with *Country File*. 'It may seem like the wrong time, but I need to talk about that meeting I had with the accountants.' She pulled out a bulging file from the bureau, dropped it on the coffee table and opened her laptop. The administration work involved in running a farm she often stated, was vast and complex. Jamie knew his mother regularly spent full afternoons on it, but he hadn't taken much interest in what she did.

'As you know,' she said, accessing the spreadsheet on her laptop, 'the last year hasn't been a great one, as far as finances are concerned. We're struggling to make those loan payments.'

Martin gave a sarcastic laugh and shook his head. 'We canna work any harder than we presently do.'

'No,' she agreed, 'Because of the changes that have come about from Brexit.' She paused and took a breath. 'Small family farms like us - and yes, we *are* a small farm, when you compare us with many others—we've been severely impacted.'

'Know all that, tha dinna have ter tell me!' interrupted Martin with a toss of his head.

'I had a good talk with the accountant,' Beth went on. 'He's suggesting that we carefully plan what we need to do, then come up with a budget for it. Then, we monitor how things are going and think about ways to diversify.'

'Not a rosy future,' said Martin with a gloomy sigh 'And now, we're paying Neil Atkinson ter do what I would normally do!'

'It's only an hour each morning and if we need him for any extra jobs, he says to just text him,' said Beth, sounding more cheerful than she probably felt. 'We'll get by. But we need to do something *different*. Something that will generate more income.'

Jamie, who had pulled out some maths homework and was listening to the conversation at the same time, piped up, 'I can work the weekends, no problem.'

'Thank you,' said his mother. 'So long as your homework doesn't suffer.'

Jamie frowned over the maths questions. He wished he'd paid attention in class when the teacher was explaining the formulae. Maybe he'd go in the other room and call Josh or Nick.

Suddenly, his father said, 'Thaz mekking heavy weather ower that, lad. Is it maths? Let's tek a look.'

Reluctantly, Jamie got up and thrust the question paper at his father. After a moment or two spent perusing the first question, Martin surprised him by reeling off the formula. When Jamie looked blank, Martin slapped the paper back at him and raised his voice. 'If tha canna understand that, well, I dinna know where tha keeps tha brains!'

'Oh Martin! Don't be mean!' Beth scolded as she saw the hurt expression on their son's face. 'I'm sure I wouldn't get it straightaway either.'

***

The following morning, Jamie met Neil coming down the Top Thorn track in Under Clough's Land Rover. He was a powerfully built young man of twenty with an affable nature, who worked efficiently, dividing his week between three or four different farms, as well as his father's poultry and mixed farm. This was the path Jamie wanted to take himself once he could leave school. He'd take the driving test as soon as he was seventeen, but until then he planned to use a tractor for travel between farms, as he could apply for his provisional tractor licence at sixteen. It seemed unlikely, in his opinion, that anyone needed mathematical skills for this kind of work, or indeed the other stuff he had to do battle with at school! He and Neil gave each other a thumbs up.

The final days of autumn passed and winter set in. Bitter winds whipped around Jamie's ears and hair, and heavy rain threatened to soak him, as he ran up the track in the mornings. He liked to time himself running for the school bus. The weather didn't bother him too much.

Sometimes he saw Neil and paused for a quick chat. The arrangement was working out well and his mother managed the rest of the routine work, with Jamie helping at weekends. He heard her say that she'd taken her name off the supply teachers' list. In any case, she never seemed to get primary teaching for which she was qualified. Instead, she'd been given random days at far-flung secondary schools.

His father was in a slightly more cheerful mood, having accepted his physical limitations. One of the casts had been removed, and he was using the crutches with great determination, emitting a burst of curses should one drop. Jamie learned to dodge out of the way of those crutches! It wouldn't be long now, before his second cast would be removed. Meanwhile, Martin immersed himself in researching farming topics online, as well as taking on routine administration work that Beth usually did. She was presently spending a large part of her day outside.

Then one morning at the beginning of December, Top Thorn Farm received some worrying news. Jamie's parents broke it to him when he arrived home from school, although he already knew through Josh who'd got a text from his brother at the end of period 5. Cattle at one of the farms that Neil Atkinson worked for had just tested positive for bovine TB. This meant that all the farms within a 4km radius needed to test their herds. As a farmer's son, Jamie knew about the routine testing of cattle that was carried out by a qualified vet every four years in the South Lakes, which was categorised as a low-risk area. Some areas in the UK were high risk and needed to test every six months. He also knew there was no cure for bovine TB. It was a respiratory disease, as in humans, and in animals it could be transmitted through nose-to-nose contact or through saliva, urine or faeces. Affected cattle had to be culled.

Martin's face looked like thunder. He had spent several hours on the phone with neighbouring farmers and an APHA officer. 'This is all we need!'

'Hopefully, we should be OK,' said his wife, trying to sound more assured than she felt.

'You're forgetting that *we* bought a bull in August from the Kilnholme sale,' he snapped, jabbing a finger at his wife as he referred to a farm that had auctioned off its entire stock, upon its owners' retirement.

Jamie was shocked by his father's outburst at his mother, especially the reference to '*we*'. 'Mum weren't even there. You bid for it,' he told his father. I was wi' yer at the auction.'

'Keep out of what doesn't concern tha!' roared Martin.

Jamie couldn't concentrate on his homework that night, nor could he engage with lessons at school the next day. He was sent to stand outside the geography lesson for being rude to the teacher when reprimanded for looking at his phone, instead of following the statistics up on the screen. He liked the subject well enough, but Miss McPherson's shrill voice grated on him, and he wished his set was being taught by the teacher they'd had last year, who taught with gusto and humour. Out in the corridor, he slumped against the wall, feeling like an idiot, especially when he heard the clickety-clack of high heels and saw the headteacher approaching. *Shit!*

'What's your name? Why aren't you in class?' she demanded. When he gave the reason, she said '*Don't let it happen again.*' At least she didn't remind him, as had Miss McPherson, that his sister had been one of the school's star students.

It was a long and dreary day; he spent both the morning break and lunch break in the library using a computer to read about TB in cattle. Unfortunately, Mr Black had another go at him over that long overdue tractor book. He muttered that he'd bring in money to pay for it. Mr Black said, 'OK, I'll accept a £5 contribution.' Remembering how old and worn the book had been, Jamie scowled and said it was ancient and not worth £5.

'It's a contribution towards the cost of replacing it

with similar, not what you think the book was worth,'
Mr Black replied, date stamping a book for a pig-tailed
year 7 girl who stood before his desk. A couple of year
10 boys, who knew Jamie because they were on his
bus, lurked in the background idly picking up
magazines from the nearby display rack and dropping
them on the floor. They sniggered.

'And you two troglodytes can depart. You're
clearly not reading.' Mr Black raised the spectacles
from his nose and glared at the boys.

'Sir, have you got a book on tractors?' asked the
taller of the two, making 'vrooom vroom!' noises.

'I'll do a search,' volunteered the student helper
who sat at the catalogue computer. 'Yes! A Short
History of Tractors in Ukrainian, by Marina
Lee…wicker,' she cried, looking up from the screen
in expectation of praise.

'Lewycka. And it's not about tractors,' sighed Mr
Black, producing a crumpled handkerchief to polish
his spectacles. They all stared at him, ready to argue.
Jamie left them to it and went off to find a vacant
computer, his mind focussed on bovine TB.

'The vet's been this afternoon and done the TB testing,' said his mother, who met him in the yard, still wearing her overalls and wellies. 'The results should be emailed back to us within a couple of days, and we'll know how many reactors we have in the herd.'

'What about Neil? Are we still having him?'

'Of course. He knows to observe all the necessary procedures, so there's no risk of spreading infection between farms. Obviously, they've tested at Under Clough as well.' Beth walked towards the house. 'I'm going in now. When you've changed, perhaps you'll feed the calves. Wear a mask when you go near the stock, there's a box of them in the porch, and disinfect your wellies. You can feed the dogs and cats as well.'

By the time Jamie had done the feeding, it was nearly dark. He whistled up the dogs, started the quad bike and roared off to check the sheep. He didn't really need to do this because his mother would have been out on the fells early that afternoon, but he just wanted a bit of time to himself. Any day now, the sheep would all be brought down off the high ground and he looked forward to being involved in the operation.

Jamie rode around the fields, only stopping to open and close gates, the bright headlights picking out glinting sheep's eyes as they scuttled out of his way. Problems did not seem to exist out here. At least he wasn't thinking about them. After half an hour or so, he made his way back to the house. Coldness stung his face and his breath came out as steam but he felt better than he had all day, and the thought of his mother's hot supper was enticing.

He drove into the yard and returned the quad bike to stand with the tractors in the shed. The soft mooing of a cow housed with the herd in the adjacent barn met his ears and suddenly the dark feelings of anxiety and dread engulfed him. What if all the cattle were TB positive? Once it got into the blood, it could spread rapidly through a herd.

CHAPTER 4

The TB testing results returned two days later, as promised. When Jamie arrived back from school, he found his father outside in the yard, leaning on crutches and smoking a cigarette. With only one plaster cast, he was much more mobile now. The single bed had gone back upstairs.

'Six cows have tested positive,' he said, 'as well as the bull. That's seven reactors. We've put them into isolation and they'll have to go away fer culling. Your mother's up to her eyeballs in form filling. Neil's been here power washing and disinfecting.'

Jamie looked into the large cow barn and saw the empty stalls nearest to the entrance. The entire building had been scrupulously cleaned, and the air was sharp and heady with disinfectant fumes. He was filled with a deep sadness for the fate of animals that

43

relied upon farmers such as themselves for their wellbeing. How many more cattle would they lose?

'Definitely not out of the woods yet,' Martin Bouthwaite declared, shaking his head and frowning as they made their way to the house. 'We'll be testing the herd again in a week.'

After two weeks, four more cows tested positive for TB. Martin said the outbreak had affected three neighbouring farms, one of which had lost over half their herd. All had bought at the Kilnholme auction, the source of the outbreak. Jamie knew farms had to routinely test and record dates of testing on each cow's passport, so that bull his father had bought must have developed its symptoms after its recorded routine test and before the sale.

He was also aware that many in the farming community believed that badgers were largely responsible for spreading the disease, but that current research was trying to disprove this idea. Thousands of badgers had been culled in recent years. As a wildlife lover, Jamie felt empathy with the badgers; he'd read an RSPCA report online about ongoing investigation and a survey sent out to farmers, vets and members of the public on the subject.

Jamie had heard his parents talk about some financial compensation being available through the government or their insurance to farmers affected by the current outbreak. His mother was busy with the paperwork, but somehow for him, it didn't remove the grief of loss for the livestock that they had reared and cared for.

***

A trip was laid on during the last week of term for year 11s wishing to visit the Careers Fair at Kendal College. Reluctantly, Jamie attended and aimlessly trailed around the various stands, having told himself in advance there would be nothing to interest him. He collected a pile of leaflets which he planned to dump in the nearest bin when they got back to school. There were courses galore on catering, computer science, business, electrical engineering, building construction, joinery and vehicle maintenance.

Even if his father was to agree to him starting work on the farm, he knew of the requirement to continue education up to the age of eighteen, which meant doing some sort of course alongside farming. But what use would any of these be? The army was there, (he sped past those characters in camouflage and heavy boots), and a few local companies were represented.

He boarded the coach returning to school, and dived into a seat near the back. Josh, chatting to a girl was in no hurry.

'Hey Jamie, saving that seat for anyone? I'll sit with you.' To his annoyance, Becca Ellis was about to drop her ample body next to him.

'Sorry Becca! That's my seat.' Nick Dixon conveniently rescued him and sat down.

'It's anybody's seat and I got here first!' Becca scowled at Nick.

But Nick ignored her. 'What did yer make of that show?' he said to Jamie. 'Only thing I fancied was the army. And that's just 'cos I could get away from home.'

Jamie knew that Nick's home was somewhat crowded, him being the oldest of five siblings. 'Yer wouldn't like the discipline, mate. It'd be worse than school.'

'Aye. And I *don't* plan to stay on there! No point in

doing another two years. It's just biding time. Doesn't always mean you've got better prospects. F'cksake! I've noticed kids who've done sixth form, now working on Tesco checkout!' Nick sighed dramatically. 'I s'pose you're still stuck on farming?'

'Aye, if me parents'll allow me. They say I should get a trade.'

'P'raps not such a bad idea. My dad's a rep for an agricultural feeds company and he says there's more small farms selling up than ever before, 'cos they can't make 'em pay. Dad has to travel a lot further ter get his orders. He says when the old farmers retire, there's no younger folk that can afford ter go into farming. Unless yer inherit a farm, and take over from parents, there's no way into farming! Even some o' those that do inherit, end up selling 'cos by then, they've moved away and got jobs. A lot o' houses are getting bought up as second homes by folks from away. It's sent property prices sky high, my dad says. Now, mebbe that's a career to get into? Selling property …'

Jamie let Nick prattle on about jobs, whilst he thought about how desperately he wanted to make Top Thorn a viable farm. *There's got to be ways.* Suddenly,

Becca's chubby face appeared over the top of the seat in front and drew close to Nick. 'Dork!' she sneered.

Nick put a hand up at either side of his head, waved his fingers and grunted a loud 'Moo!' then stuck out his tongue. Jamie nearly choked himself, trying not to laugh as Becca slid back in disgust.

***

'Did you find the careers fair interesting?' Beth Bouthwaite closed her laptop and pushed a pile of paperwork aside, in readiness to prepare supper.

Jamie padded over to the sink in his socks to wash his hands. He'd just come in from the feeding chores. 'Alreet.'

'Any courses that you fancied? Joinery? Engineering?'

'None that I could relate t' farming.'

'They must have business administration courses?'

'Aye, I did see that.'

'Farming's a business, Jamie. It's as much about balancing books as it is about raising livestock and driving tractors around.' She waved a hand at the pile of papers and sighed heavily.

'I could've taken business studies as a GCSE, but no lads signed up for it.' He remembered that he still had the college leaflets in his bag. Perhaps he'd take a quick look before chucking them away. Even so, a business course with a load of girls did *not* appeal. Sticking in his earbuds to listen to music, he left the kitchen and headed for his room.

That night, he dreamed he was at a farm sale. It was so real. He heard the auctioneer's rasping voice calling out the bids: 'Who'll give me six? Who'll give me eight? Do I hear ten over there?' He assumed it was the Kilnholme sale last summer. Everything was going under the hammer, livestock, tractors, implements and even the working dogs …Wait a second … didn't that brown and white collie look like Toby?

'No!' he cried out, recognising the farm was Top Thorn! There was the large barn… and the house. People, whom he didn't recognise wearing expensive country gear, stood in the yard grinning. He smelt and saw curls of cigar smoke. No sign of his parents. Jamie searched for a familiar face and found none. An elderly voice was declaring that just like coal mining, farming was redundant now. He writhed and moaned aloud as he tried to change the dream. Wide awake, he sat up, sobbing, drenched in sweat and his heart thumping.

It was only a dream, but he tossed and turned for what seemed like hours before he fell asleep again.

***

End of term heralded the prospect of two glorious weeks without school. But during their assembly year 11 were warned that mock GCSE exams would start during the first week back, and they were advised to make revision timetables for the Christmas holidays. Jamie and Josh groaned as they listened with half an ear to their Year Head's advice. Both could think of far better things to do over the holidays.

Jamie's sister Sally returned from university. She was sitting at the kitchen table when he got home from school on the last day of term. 'Hey little bro!' She raised sparkling blue eyes to greet him, and her mouth creased into a grin. It always irritated him when she teased him with 'little' because at nearly six foot, he towered way above her. Responding with a scowl, he helped himself to three chocolate biscuits from the open packet, and went off to change, taking the stairs two at a time.

His parents were delighted to have their bright and bubbly daughter back in the fold. Sally was in her first year, studying veterinary medicine at Manchester. A brilliant student at school, she had excelled at everything she touched, even playing first violin in the orchestra, so they were justifiably proud of her. Jamie had always felt inferior and unable to match her academic accomplishments, so he hadn't really tried. Now, she seemed to chatter non-stop about her new friends. *Boring*, he thought. It also appeared that she had a boyfriend called Milo, so it was 'Milo did this', 'Milo says that' and 'Milo and I went...' Jamie looked at his father and rolled his eyes. Martin, who was at last free from plaster and in a much lighter mood, reciprocated the eye-rolling.

Christmas was rapidly approaching; Sally and her mother spent the best part of an afternoon decorating a Christmas tree and putting sprigs of berried holly behind the pictures. Despite having been away from the farm for three months, Sally was more than happy to pull her weight in sharing the chores, and early each morning donned outdoor overalls.

'Losing ten cattle plus the bull to TB, must have been horrible,' she said to Jamie when they were mucking out together.

'Too reet.' He didn't want to talk about it. The pain of loss still ached.

'Not to mention Dad's accident. I bet he's been a lousy patient.'

'Too reet.' Jamie cut open a bale of clean straw. 'He's just got a knee brace thing now, but yer shoulda seen him wi' both legs in plaster! And in a wheelchair.'

On Christmas Eve, whilst enjoying a festive meal, red candles glowing and glasses of sparkling wine on the table, Sally started a conversation on her ideas how to make the farm more viable for the future. 'You could create a static caravan park, have some shepherds' huts, or better still, convert one of the barns into self-catering accommodation,' she declared, raising her glass to take a drink. 'Think of the revenue that would bring.'

'And where would the money come from to do it?'

countered Martin, smiling fondly at his blonde pony tailed daughter.

'Grants might be available! You could apply to one of these rural help agencies,' Sally told him. 'Maybe we could turn all the barns into holiday accommodation?'

'I'd prefer ter carry on actual farming,' muttered Jamie.

'And your definition of that?' countered Sally.

'Raising and looking after animals. That's farming. I'd hate strangers staying just across t' yard and behaving as if they owned t' place, parking their cars in t' way and tramping everywhere, leaving gates open!'

The others smiled at his passion. 'The holiday accommodation could be for those who are interested in real rural life and don't see the countryside as a theme park,' Sally went on, helping herself to a generous spoonful of cranberry sauce and smearing it over her pork fillet. 'And if you still want to keep cattle, you could put up one of those metal buildings, specially designed for purpose. Research what grants exist, Dad!'

'Very few, Sal,' he said quietly.

All of them, including Jamie, who had tried unsuccessfully to use the excuse of needing to be up early for the chores, went out for Midnight Mass at the village church. It was a traditional Christmas custom in their rural community. The congregation was swelled by second homeowners and those in self-catering rentals, here to experience a Cumbrian Christmas; several shiny Jaguars and BMWs sat on the church car park. There was no sign of the Atkinson family. Part way through the service, a dozen well-oiled revellers trooped in from the Farmers' Arms, adding hearty but discordant voices to the carol singing. Jamie and Sally nudged each other and giggled.

Once the essential farm work was done, Christmas Day passed in a haze of over-eating, gift exchanging and TV entertainment. On Boxing Day evening, the family settled in the living room made cosy by the blazing log fire. The parents sat in their armchairs, whilst Jamie and Sally occupied the sofa. *Die Hard,* which everyone had seen at least once, was about to begin on TV, when they had an unexpected visitor. It was Neil Atkinson, whom they were more used to seeing in work attire, now looking quite handsome in a smart checked shirt, new jeans and reeking of aftershave. He put a tray of eggs on the kitchen table and carried some cans of beer and a box of chocolates into the living room.

'Come in Neil, and sit down,' Beth waved him in with a smile and clicked the TV's remote to switch it off.

Neil hadn't been needed since Jamie had broken up school and Sally was at home for the holiday. 'Hope yer dinna mind. I've cum t' escape 'ouseful o' aunts n' uncles, n' cousins. There's a scrabble game ga'an on, o' which kid brother's shamelessly beating everyone,' he said in his deep soft voice. Neil's accent and dialect always broadened when he was with his native farming community. They all did it unconsciously, but at school Jamie found himself moderating his speech when talking to teachers.

Martin Bouthwaite was pleased to see the curly-haired young man who'd been so helpful during the last few months. They pulled open some cans. Jamie looked hopeful, but no one offered him a beer, so he started on the chocolates. He dragged out another chair, because Neil had sat down next to Sally on the sofa and was asking questions about her university life. Jamie was surprised that she answered as briefly as possible without being rude. Normally, she would jump at any opportunity to talk on this subject. Neil coloured, as he was obviously trying to think of topics that would interest her. 'D'yer get any good bands coming t' do gigs at uni?'

'Yeah, sometimes.'

Neil tried another question, to which she gave a perfunctory reply. Jamie thought he looked as if he was about to try another subject when Sally smoothed back her sleek curtain of blonde hair and got up with an apologetic smile. 'Sorry Neil, I've just remembered that I'm expecting a WhatsApp call from a friend.'

Jamie saw disappointment in Neil's brown eyes as they followed her shapely figure leaving the room. Neil fancied her, and Jamie would make sure he'd tease Sally about it the following day.

But for now, he joined the conversation around the fireside. It revolved around farming topics. Neil was thinking about buying a machine that would convert his tractor so it could perform several different tasks. Tossing a log onto the fire and watching the sparks catch and crackle for a moment, Martin said, 'A versatile piece of kit Neil, but wouldn't the investment be a large one for yer?'

Neil shrugged and said that sometimes you had to make investments in your business to develop the potential. 'I need t' offer summat more than just me labour. Me favver's agreed t' help wi' deposit, and the bank's happy t' gi' me a loan.' He set his empty can down on the table. Jamie noticed his parents briefly glance at each other. He knew the Atkinson farm was more profitable than Top Thorn.

Jamie walked outside with Neil to his black Freelander. The night air was thick with fast flying snowflakes; the first snow of this winter, and it was already sticking where it landed, on the ground and on the barn roof. He wanted to ask about getting into agricultural contracting, but Neil opened his car door, and remarked with studied casualness, 'D'yer think yer sister might still be here f't New Year?'

'She hasn't said.' Jamie stuck his hands in his pockets. It was freezing. 'But I can't see her going back before. Why yer wanna know?'

'Oh, just wondered if she's any thoughts on ga'an t' Young Farmers' New Year's Eve do.' Neil got in behind the wheel and stuck his key into the ignition.

'Happen yer'll have t' ask her.'

'Happen I will. See yer, Jamie.' He turned the ignition, and the engine started up.

'Aye, I might cum ower t' yours and see Josh, tomorrow, like.'

After Neil had rumbled out of the yard, skidding towards the track, Jamie remained outside for a few minutes, marvelling at how the falling snowflakes lit up the dark night. He imagined running through the flying snow, high up on the fells. He loved the feeling of freedom that running created in him.

Across the yard came a gentle moan from a cow as it shuffled in its stall and he thought about the dogs sleeping in their kennel with half an ear awake for any unfamiliar sound, and in his mind's eye he pictured the sheep, crouching by walls for shelter. In the morning, he might be out there taking bales of hay to them. He saw himself throwing them off the quad bike's trailer and the hungry sheep coming towards him from all directions.

But how much longer would this be his life? There was all this talk about farmers diversifying. His parents seemed so touchy on the subject. But surely, they must be thinking about it. Even Neil was making a heavy investment. He recalled his words: *I need t'offer summat more than just me labour.*

As Jamie shivered and walked back to the house, the thought came to him: *What can I offer to help Top Thorn?* The disasters of the last two months flashed before him. First his father's accident, followed by losing cattle to TB. How long would it take to build the herd back? They had always bred their own bull, but his father had bought one in and it had turned out to be a big mistake.

CHAPTER 5

Next morning, the outside world lay blanketed in snow. Jamie and his father, who was driving again, since the last plaster cast had been removed, chugged off by tractor with bales for the sheep. Sally and their mother mucked out the cows. By nine o'clock when they all trooped into the kitchen for a cooked breakfast, the sun had appeared and the sky was a brilliant blue, adorned with just a solitary cloud that looked like a puff of whitey grey smoke.

Martin tuned into a news programme on the local radio station. The presenter was announcing details of social events taking place over the next few days, and Jamie suddenly remembered his conversation with Neil. He looked at Sally as she poured herself a mug of tea.

'Will yer still be here f't New Year? Neil was

asking if…'

'Oh, was he?' she said, grabbing a handful of cutlery from the drawer. 'Ooh Mum, could I have two rashers, please?

'He's ganna contact yer,' Jamie went on. 'About the Young Farmers' do on New Year's Eve.'

'That'll be a posh one. I believe they're holding it at the Elter Valley Hotel this time,' said Beth, slapping plates of bacon and eggs onto the table.

Sally said nothing as she proceeded to butter a slice of toast. They all looked at her and smiled.

'Think he might fancy you!' sang out Jamie and received a scowl from his sister.

'Who'd want to spend New Year's Eve with that lot? They'll all be off their faces and well trolleyed by nine o'clock!' she declared.

'Bet Neil won't be, if you're there,' said Jamie, smearing egg yolk over his bacon before shovelling it into his mouth.

'Have you any plans for New Year's Eve, Sally?' asked her mother.

'Yeah, me and two of my old schoolmates, Karen and Rachel are going to Carlisle. It's an open-air gig.

Rachel's dad's driving.

'Neil's ganna be disappointed, that's for sure.' Jamie teased her by making his voice sound tragic.

'Too bad!' Sally gave him a playful shove, almost causing him to spill his tea. He shoved her back and laughed. Privately, he thought that getting 'trolleyed' with a crowd of lively young farmers sounded like fun.

***

The snow had cleared from the roads by midday and after lunch, Jamie cycled down the road to Under Clough, the Atkinsons' farm. Josh greeted him in the yard.

'Hey, mate! Yer know I applied fer apprenticeship with R V Kelly?'

'Agricultural engineers in Kendal. Aye,' said Jamie, jumping off his bike. 'Yer ganna tell me yer've got an interview?'

'Aye!' Josh could hardly keep still in his excitement. 'I won't be t' only one for it, not by a long chalk,' he said. 'There'll be lads that's already done a year in college, so me brother says. I'll have to gen up on interview techniques. Remember that careers woman who came into school last term? She was on about on how ter handle job interviews.'

'When's the interview?'

'Third of January, quarter to eleven.'

'Huh, yer'll nail it, mate!' Jamie knew how Josh loved tinkering about with farm machinery and he had fixed a car that wouldn't start for one of the teachers on the school car park last term. That job would be perfect for him. He was genuinely pleased for Josh, but wished his own future was as clear.

'What'll be, will be, as me mam says. And I'll need good GCSEs, so me predicted grades are important.' Josh tossed his head, attempting to look wise. 'Anyways, what you ganna do when we finish school in t' summer?'

'Thought yer knew. I wanna work on't farm and do a bit o' contracting. If I can work wi' me favver, then me mother can go back ter teaching.'

'Is that what she wants ter do?'

'If a job came up in a local primary school, I think she'd apply.' *If Mum's teaching, they'll have to let me work on the farm*, he thought.

'But hey mate, I don't see why yer shouldna be able ter mek a living from farm contracting. Me brother does well enough outta it. He'd p'raps help yer start.'

'Aye, that's what I'm hoping.'

Josh slapped him on the back. 'It'll work out mate.' Then he drew Jamie's attention to two large, old sledges leaned up against a wall. 'Eh, look what I've found in one o' t barns! Must've been used years ago fer tekking hay bales out, or summat. Let's have some fun!'

They dragged the sledges up the nearest hill and spent the best part of two hours racing each other down the slopes. They ended up with a snowball fight that got decidedly rough, disintegrating into a rugby tackle. Finally, red faced and wet, they trudged happily back to the farmyard and into the house, kicking off their snowy boots and throwing aside dripping coats. A wonderful aroma of baking pervaded the kitchen.

Mrs Atkinson, an attractive woman with green highlighted hair, dangly earrings and arms floured up to her elbows, had the local radio station on and was bopping to Franz Ferdinand. Josh rolled his eyes at Jamie as she paused to draw breath and laugh at the lads. 'Looks like yer both forgot yer waterproofs. Get out o' those wet things! Josh, find Jamie something dry ter wear.' A plate piled high with oven warm scones together with a dish of butter and a pot of raspberry jam awaited them when they entered the kitchen a few minutes later. Jamie's mouth watered as he took a seat and reached for a plate.

Mr Atkinson came in and washed his hands at the sink. Of a stocky build, he was several inches shorter than his sons. 'How's tha ga'an on lads? What's crack 't Top Thorn?' His brown eyes twinkled as he joined them at the table. As always, it struck Jamie how different Josh's father was to his own father. He made them laugh with his corny jokes and soon the scones had disappeared. Jamie was relieved that Neil didn't show up because he felt bad about knowing Sally's New Year plans. He'd find another opportunity to talk to him about agricultural contracting.

Darkness was drawing in as Jamie cycled home in a borrowed pair of tracksuit pants and his own soaking wet clothing in a carrier bag hanging from the handlebars. It also contained a can of beer Josh had given him. He'd had a great afternoon. As he skidded to a halt in the yard, he saw Sally coming out of the barn, the dogs following her with tails wagging. He guessed that she'd just fed them.

He told her about Josh's forthcoming interview. 'Good for him. You should think seriously about what you're going to be doing next year,' she said. Jamie thought she sounded a lot like the school careers teacher.

'Year 11 just seems to fly by and before you know where you are, it's the end of May and you're starting the exams,' Sally went on. 'Josh is right to make his decisions now.'

'Sure. He knows what he wants to do and so do I. I wanna work on't farm with Favver and contract out like Neil.' He heard her give an exasperated sigh as he wheeled his bike over to the tractor shed.

There was less than a week left before the start of term and Jamie hadn't even started revising for the mocks. He'd kept putting it off, but Sally caught him after the morning chores were done and suggested looking through his revision files. 'Even if you're not going to stay on at school, which is fine, it's your choice,' she said, 'but hey, why not take the opportunity of giving these exams your best effort and see what you're capable of?'

Reluctantly, he brought the files downstairs, and they spent a few hours on chemistry and physics. By lunchtime, she had tested him, and he felt that he'd made surprisingly good progress. After supper, they looked at some past GCSE maths papers and the following day he brought out his biology, geography, and English files. Even those maths equations looked easier.

She talked about her own system of revision, in which she gave herself little edible treats on completion of tasks. With chocolates and sweets still lurking around from Christmas, this sounded doable. 'Borrow one of those Shakespeare CDs or the poetry ones they have in the English department,' she suggested. 'Download it onto your phone, and listen on your headphones whilst you're out running.'

Having an older sister home for the holiday wasn't too bad, even if she did go on like a teacher about revision. He found himself relenting. There were six months of school left. It would be preferable to finish with some decent results rather than rubbish ones. Jamie was almost sorry, when on January fourth, Sally returned to Manchester.

Three days later found him seated in the school hall with a hundred and twenty other students, waiting for the invigilator to start the physics exam. The heating had been on at a low setting to save energy during the holidays, and it was chilly. Because of this, they were allowed to wear their coats. He flexed his cold fingers and glanced over at Josh. They grinned at each other and gave the thumbs up sign. It didn't go unnoticed by the invigilator who barked out a sharp reprimand. An hour and a half later, the students streamed out of the hall. Whilst some of his peers, including Nick Dixon, could be heard swearing and grumbling to each other, Jamie was feeling quietly confident. It had been OK!

Most of the mock exams were doled out during that first week back in school after Christmas, with just geography, French and design technology remaining to be taken Monday and Tuesday of the next week. Jamie and Josh, both having prepared well for the exams, were in high spirits as they kicked a football around with some rowdy year 10 lads whilst waiting for the school bus on Friday afternoon. They were not friends of theirs. In fact, last term, these two had caused a fair bit of trouble on the bus, and at this moment the only reason Jamie tolerated them was the football.

The taller of the two lads was Liam Hodgson, and he should really have been in year 11 but had been held back to do year 10 again. Pushing Jamie roughly aside, he proceeded to board the bus in front of him. Refusing to be outdone, Jamie snatched the bag that hung loosely off the boy's shoulder and, with a laugh, hurled it back onto the muddy verge. 'Come on lads, that's enough horseplay!' shouted the bus duty teacher.

When Jamie jumped off the bus at Top Thorn, he noticed threatening, leaden grey clouds in the darkening sky, and the first heavy drops of rain landed on his head and shoulders. The wind had picked up, pulling greedily at the branches of a clump of pine trees, and making a whooshing sound. He recognised the signs of an impending storm and hurried down the track to the house.

'It's ganna be a bad un.' His father, clad in filthy overalls, met him in the yard. 'We've heard on t' radio that it's red alert category. I've already done t' feeding. Let's git oursels inside.'

CHAPTER 6

Jamie awoke to hear the storm howling furiously around the house and muffled barks from the dogs as well as grunts from disturbed cattle. There was something crashing around the yard. *What could that be?* His father had been right about the calibre of this storm. It was wild! When he was younger, he'd thrilled to these freaks of weather, but now he feared the destruction that could be caused and danger to livestock. Groping for his phone on the bedside cabinet, he checked the time. The neon screen read 3.50.

He got out of bed and pulled the curtain aside to look through his window, but the pitch-black darkness revealed nothing except fierce rods of rain. Feeling for the light switch on the wall, he flicked it and found that the power was off. And then, glancing back to the window he saw the narrow beam of a torch down in the yard and knew his father was out there.

Searching around by torchlight for the clothes he'd shed last night, he pulled them on over his T-shirt and boxers. Torch in hand, he rushed onto the landing and almost bumped into his mother. 'I'll go out wi' Favver.'

'No, you will *not*,' she said. 'He's only making a quick check. There's nothing any of us can do right now. Go back to bed and we'll look at the situation when it's light.'

He compromised by going down to the warm kitchen to wait for his father. Beth lit some candles. After about ten minutes, Martin Bouthwaite returned. 'All t' cattle are safe, but the roof's gone on t' calves' barn,' he reported, throwing off his waterproof jacket.

The calves were housed in a low structure with a corrugated iron roof, at the back of the main barn. Nothing could be done until daylight, when the storm's full impact would be properly assessed. Although the family returned to their beds, nobody slept. They were glad when first light dawned. The sky glowed luminously red, but the worst of the storm had calmed.

The wooden panel comprising the back wall of the tractor shed had come down, and loose tarpaulin sheets that were stored in it blew and flapped around in the wind. Jamie went out with his father to look for the missing roof. Amazingly, it had blown across two fields, and they found one dead and two bleating and traumatised sheep trapped beneath it. They came back on a tractor with lifting gear and raised it sufficiently to pull the sheep out, carefully checking the live ones for injury. Fortunately, the rest of the flock had escaped to the other side of the field.

There was no way this rusting piece of bent corrugated iron was going to form a roof again. 'It should really have been replaced years ago, and it's now damaged beyond redemption,' said Martin. 'Best we can do now as a temporary measure, will be ter git some tarps fastened onto t' wooden support beams. 'Least, they're still up.'

They spent the morning working on this job until they used their last tarpaulin. Whilst his father sat in the tractor cab, keeping steady the hydraulic extending arm, Jamie crouched in the bucket and nailed the tarpaulin onto the wooden beams that were fixed close to the wall. He was pleased to be doing such an important and useful job. It made him feel like a man! Below him, the calves eyed him with curiosity.

After lunch, Len Atkinson and his sons arrived to see how much damage Top Thorn had sustained. Their power was also off so the generator was supplying electricity to their barns. A tree had come down, blocking access to their back track; Neil would bring the chain saw out to deal with that tomorrow. Otherwise, Under Clough was OK.

Martin Bouthwaite, whilst giving an air of self-sufficiency, had to appreciate the help of their friends when Josh and Neil hauled a big tarpaulin out of the back of their Land Rover. 'This'll strengthen what yer've already done,' said Neil.

Three of them pulled the tarpaulin tight at the lower end of the sloping roof, whilst Jamie and his father secured the ends. Then Martin brought the trailer round and Jamie loaded it up with a pile of sturdy wooden planks. These were next nailed at intervals over the calves' new roof for extra firmness.

The job was completed, and they all stood back in satisfaction to survey it. Len Atkinson mentioned the name of a decent roofing contractor that he'd recently used. Martin noted the name, but Jamie knew all too well they didn't have the finances at the moment. They could repair the back of the tractor shed themselves and maybe after the September sheep sales they could think about doing something more permanent to the calves' accommodation. In any case, Jamie was aware this batch of calves would be sold in the late spring.

After lunch, they discovered a more serious problem; the roof of the main barn had deteriorated further. Several ridge tiles had become displaced because of crumbling mortar, and some slates had also slipped out of place. It had received no attention when the conversion from diary was made several years ago. 'The whole roof needs replacing, but we'll just have t' get the worst parts fettled fer now,' Martin told Jamie.

Another fall of snow arrived on Sunday afternoon and the power remained off until Monday morning. The bus on its way to Mereside Academy was buzzing with complaints that it should have stayed off longer so that school would have been closed. But at least they had an excuse for uncompleted homework.

As the driver pulled up at Rose Bank, a row of shabby cottages which was the last stop before the school, the two year 10 lads were fighting with each other on the pavement. They carried on despite the arrival of their bus. The little sister of one of them hastened aboard. Everyone started banging on the windows and making catcalls. Reducing the volume of his 'Queen's Greatest Hits' CD, the driver opened the door and yelled at them to get on the bus now, otherwise they would be left. Dishevelled, with snow in their hair and ties askew at their necks, the boys leapt aboard. Liam Hodgson, who was first, bounded clumsily down the aisle, not seeing one of Jamie's long legs sticking out between the seats. He tripped and, after picking himself up from the floor, turned aggressively to Jamie and swore at him.

Jamie hadn't intended to trip Hodgson and had been about to apologise. Abruptly, he changed his mind and said menacingly, 'Watch yer step, *oaf*!'

The other students, apart from two year 9 girls who had mirrors out checking their make-up, made encouraging noises, hoping for another fight. As

Hodgson moved forward and opened his mouth to retaliate, the driver roared, 'Unless you lot shut up and sit down, this bus is going nowhere, and you can get off!' They all fell silent and the bus moved off.

After lunch, Jamie strolled along the wide corridor that led from the dining hall and was about to ascend the library stairs intending to look at some homework, when a bunch of laughing boys came charging down towards him. They had been evicted from the library for throwing books off the shelves; the ringleader was Liam Hodgson. He carelessly barged into Jamie, who pushed him aside with the word '*Oaf!*'

'Oaf yerself! Farm lad!' Hodgson turned to his three mates and crowed, 'His farm's got mad cow disease.' Year 10's didn't usually challenge year 11's. A few sniggers erupted.

'You know nowt. Don't mek false accusations.' Jamie's hand was on the banister. He took in Hodgson's somewhat dishevelled state; the grubby shirt collar, the muddied trouser knees.

'Mad cow! Mad cow!' Hodgson hissed. 'And yer favver's a crap farmer. Crap farmer!'

'Ignore him Jamie, he yatters out o' his arse,' a

voice came from below them. It was Josh.

'Crap farmer!' repeated Hodgson and turned to his companions with a smirk. 'His local pub's called Farmers' Arms. Bet his favver gets hammered.' His followers took the cue and laughed because it was expected of them.

Jamie dropped his bag and sprang into action, grabbing the boy around his throat. He had him secure in one of the Cumbrian wrestling holds that he'd learned from the sport. The others all drew in their breath. A sixth form girl, trying to get down the stairs told them to pack it in, but Jamie took no notice. He just held onto Hodgson. Someone got their phone out and started recording. A small crowd had gathered. 'I'll let yer go when yer tek back all that rubbish yer've been mouthing,' he snarled close to Hodgson's ear.

''T'is true!' Spotty faced Billy Beaty, whose voice was on the verge of breaking, leaned close and Jamie caught a faint whiff of animals.

'Shuddup Beaty,' said Josh. 'Yer a twat.'

'Aye, keep yer snout out, Beaty. *Your* favver mucks out pigs.' Jamie still held onto the kicking Hodgson.

'Bummers yuz two!' gasped Hodgson, trying to free himself.

'Bummers!' repeated Beaty and stood clear of Josh, just in case he was grabbed.

'Take your hands off that boy! Bouthwaite, my office *now!*' The thunderous voice of Mr Wilkins, the deputy head, known to all as Wilko, made everyone jump. Students and staff alike always maintained that you could hear Wilko shout from one end of the school to the other. 'And I'll take that, thank you.' He held his hand out for the phone. 'The rest of you except Hodgson and Beaty, buzz off!'

Jamie stood outside the deputy's office, which was located back down the corridor. He felt the discomfort of a bruised shin where Hodgson had kicked him. The minutes slowly ticked by, and he avoided eye contact as students coming out of the dining hall looked at him. Everyone knew you only stood outside this door if you were in trouble. He pretended to read noticeboards. Finally, he heard the familiar clonk, clonk of Wilko's hard-soled shoes striding over the polished wooden blocked floor and keys jingling, as he unlocked the door. First, glancing over his shoulder, he quickly followed the deputy into his office.

It was a small room, having been converted from a former staff toilet. Housing an untidy desk upon which stood the inevitable computer screen, two chairs and a tall metal cabinet from which files bulged, it had an opaque glazed window. Jamie stood and waited, but he wasn't invited to sit.

'H'm, Jamie Bouthwaite, year 11.' Wilko was sifting through papers and pamphlets piled in a wire tray on his desk. With a flourish, he swept them into the waste bin. 'How do you think you faired in the mocks?'

Jamie stared at the man's expressionless face and the pale eyes behind the heavy rimmed spectacles. He had expected a harsh telling off. This was a surprise. 'Er… All right, sir, I think I've done all right.'

And then the lecture that he anticipated was delivered. It was the worst he'd ever received.

CHAPTER 7

Jamie barely took in the severe reprimand that exploded into his ears. It featured his 'disgraceful behaviour' that had been 'displayed for all and sundry' but he only heard the volume and the shape of words bouncing around him. Finally, Wilko took a deep breath, sat back in his chair, and folded his arms.

'Why let yourself down now?' he said quietly.

'I don't know.' Jamie stared at the dark grey resin floor. 'It just happened, sir. You might say he provoked me. Said stuff about our farm...and my father, that wasn't true.'

'Whether true or not, we have to deflect such insults without resorting to violence. Self-control, Jamie – learn it! Otherwise, you'll find yourself constantly in conflict and fights. It will get you absolutely nowhere.'

'Yes sir. I mean, no, sir.'

'Detention at morning break tomorrow. My office. You can write one side of A4 on self-control. *And*, I recommend you apologise to Liam Hodgson for attacking him as soon as possible. *And* he might even apologise to you for his silly taunts. I don't want to suspend you but if there's a parental complaint, I may have to. He may be your age, but remember he's in a lower year group. You get me?'

'Yes, sir.'

'Now go, get out of my sight!'

Shouldering his backpack, Jamie nearly ran all the way up to his form room on the top floor for afternoon registration and just made it before the tutor closed his laptop. Last period of the day was French, and he caught up with Josh walking to the MFL corridor. 'Bet yer got a reet bollockin'.'

'Too reet. Anyways, where did that pratt Hodgson get his lies from? That's what I'd like ter know. Not you and your family, surely?' The words were out before Jamie could stop himself.

'Jamie man, yer crazy!' Josh dashed on through the door, caught up with a pretty dark-haired girl and sat down beside her.

'Bon apres-midi, mes garçons et filles!' Their French teacher, who was also head of MFL, had a strong Geordie accent. Sometimes her lessons were spiced up with laughs, but she had a tough side and was strict about homework being handed in. Jamie failed to follow her jokes in French or any part of the lesson that afternoon. Instead, he focussed on the view through the window of sheep-filled fields sloping down to the lakeshore, and watched a quad bike buzzing around. *Wish I was out there*. And now, he had the threat of suspension hanging over him, like a dark and heavy cloak. He hardly dared imagine what his parents would say. The last thing he wanted to do was to apologise to Hodgson, but supposed he'd better do it.

'Haven't yer heard of 'jungle telegraph? That's what me mam says when fake information goes flying around. Or it goes on Snapchat. Where that bullshit came from, f'ck knows!' Josh said, increasing his pace when Jamie attempted to catch up with him at the end of the lesson. 'There's no way or reason for any gossip coming from *my family*.'

'Sorry, mate. I were rattled.'

Josh slowed down and grunted acceptance of the apology, and then told Jamie that after he'd gone to wait outside Wilko's room, the librarian had come down complaining about books being chucked around by Hodgson and his mates. Apparently, this must have been just before Jamie's altercation with them. Josh had heard Wilko and Mr Black doling out shelf tidying detentions in the library for the rest of the week.

Whilst they queued for the bus at the bottom of the school drive, Jamie spotted Liam Hodgson, head bent over his phone and without his mate. Remembering Wilko's advice not to let the fight escalate any further, he took a deep breath and ambled down the line until he stood right next to the lad. *Better get it over with*. He made a throat clearing noise.

'Not *you*,' Hodgson grunted, only half raising his eyes from the small screen. 'Don't need any mair trouble at t' moment.'

'Me neither,' said Jamie. 'Er look, I'm sorry fer grabbing yer, like.'

Hodgson shrugged, still not looking up. 'Huh. But yer just got caught, didn't yer? Yer wouldna be sorry otherwise.' There was the hint of a jeer in his tone. 'Mind, I never said nowt about yer tripping me up this morning on't bus. Could've done.'

'Look, that wasn't meant, and I nearly apologised but yer gave me a reet mouthful.'

'Whatever.'

'You still told lies about my family's farm. We don't have mad cow and never have done. Where d'yer hear that crap from? Mad cow or BSE, ter use its proper name, were a terrible disease that happened all ower t' country, years before we were born. Fer *your* information what our farm had were some cases of TB. *Not mad cow*. It weren't just our farm, there were others that had more cases. And I didn't like what yer said about me favver. It's *defamation*. But maybe that's too big a word for *you*!' Jamie's chest tightened as his temper rose.

Hodgson glanced up from his screen but said nothing.

'Put it this way,' Jamie fought to sound calm. 'You wouldn't like it if I bad-mouthed your favver.'

Hodgson gulped and suddenly faced him. 'You try it!' Squaring his shoulders up to Jamie, he continued,

'Yer think yer better'n us, don't yer? You and yer bummer mate, Atkinson. Yer favvers've got their own farms. Yer well set up.'

'We *don't* think we're better. Yer got that wrong.' Once again, Jamie's temper ignited but he was determined not to take the bait.

'Nah, yer got guaranteed jobs when yer leave school. Nowt ter worry aboot.' Hodgson dropped his phone into a blazer pocket and gestured back towards the school drive. 'I've got another year at this crap spot. And then what? Nowt.'

'Look,' said Jamie, as he saw the bus approaching. 'I've apologised to yer, *and* I've a detention from Wilko, but *you've* not apologised ter me fer bad-mouthing me favver.'

'F'cksake, whatever!' Hodgson hoisted his bag onto his shoulder and turned away.

Jamie wasn't satisfied that he'd received an apology, but it was probably the best he would get. The main thing was he'd apologised, as Wilko had recommended. He guessed that the other boy nursed some kind of stupid grudge against him because he lived on a farm. The queue was moving, and they both went to board the bus.

He relayed the conversation to Josh after Hodgson got off at his stop. 'He's jealous of us both because we're from farming families, but more resentful ter me, fer some weird reason.'

'Forget it, mate. He'll git ower it.'

Next morning, Jamie learned the results of his mocks, on account of which he was moving into higher sets for several subjects. Whilst it cheered him up and boosted his ego, he worried about keeping up with the work at this level. His mother was very pleased and gave him two twenty-pound notes along with his usual pocket money earned from helping on the farm, but his father merely gave a nod that might have indicated approval. To his great relief, he was not suspended from school. That would have meant a lot of trouble with his father!

The weather turned mild again at the beginning of February and the Bouthwaite flocks remained on the lower ground ready for lambing in the spring. They couldn't take any risks and needed to check them every day. The thaw had made much of the land soft and muddy, worsened by water coming down from the higher fells. Some dry-stone walls had collapsed, and Martin set about making repairs. Although his fractures had recovered remarkably well, he grumbled that his knee still gave him 'gip' and he reluctantly engaged Neil. This turned out to be a wise decision, because Neil, who held last year's Young Farmers' championship trophy for dry-stone walling, was fast and competent.

One drizzly February afternoon, after the bus dropped him off, Jamie was walking down the track when he spotted a sheep lying on its back. Knowing that sometimes a ewe heavy in lamb might stumble and be unable to get up, he ran over to take a look. He'd heard his father and other farmers use the term 'liggin' kessin' when sheep got into this situation. It was moving its legs, obviously trying to right itself. This was a good sign. He flung down his bag, got hold of the front and back legs and attempted to swing it over, hoping the ewe would be able to upright itself.

Then, to his horror and disgust, he saw that one eye was gone and blood running from the empty socket down the woolly face. Looking up into the sky, he spied a couple of crows drifting to and fro, cawing. He swore viciously at them. Not wanting to leave the poor ewe to the mercy of those horrible predators, he pulled out his phone to call his father.

Luckily, Martin was not too far away and within ten minutes, was with him. He brought antiseptic and bathed the struggling ewe's eye socket. Between them, they got it onto its feet and into the trailer. Once in the farmyard, they put it into a little covered pen they kept as a 'hospital ward' for livestock. It would stay there until the eye socket had healed.

'There's some folks that think it's less work looking after sheep than cattle,' said his father with a short laugh, as they walked towards the house. 'But yer constantly monitoring them for things like t' fluke, as well as parasites, lameness, coughing, checking their teeth, *and* all t' rest. Then yer've got dipping. On top o' it all, yer've got bloody predators like craws ter contend wi'! They'll ga'an fer yer lambs at every opportunity.'

Jamie nodded in agreement and experienced something close to being treated as an equal. In finding that poor ewe, he'd done something right, although he'd received no praise.

Jamie was a junior member of the local Young Farmers' branch and along with Josh, enjoyed the many rural activities, competitions and sporting events on offer. They'd both competed in Cumbrian wrestling and last summer, had represented their local branch at an area sports day, Jamie having won a rosette for the under 18s.

Now, he looked forward to becoming a senior member and taking part in more activities that connected him to the farming world that he loved. He'd attended dry stone walling and stock judging events last year, and had got his name down for this year's tug o' war team. In February their branch ran a trip to watch Carlisle United play Newcastle United and it was a thrilling way to celebrate Josh's sixteenth birthday, especially as their team won.

Jamie was envious that Josh had applied for his provisional tractor licence. R V Kelly had offered him an apprenticeship, conditional on his GCSE results, so Josh was riding high. It was a prestigious company and he boasted to all his mates at school. And Sophie, the dark-haired girl in their maths set was interested in him. He told Jamie they were texting each other.

Jamie would have to wait until he turned sixteen in mid-March before he could apply for his provisional licence. *Another month and I'll be legal*, he was thinking to himself one Saturday morning, after finishing his chores. And then the idea came to him. *Why not get a bit of practice driving around the farm on one of the tractors?*

His father took a relaxed view of him driving on flat areas of the farm, as long as he was under supervision. But on that damp and sunless morning, Martin had gone off to inspect a dyke on another distant part of the land, and Beth was shopping in Kendal. He drove the old John Deere around the farmyard for a while and practised operating the hydraulic bucket over a heap of gravel. It was noisy and stupidly slow. His father often said with pride that this tractor had been fitted with more heads than an old broom. Then he put it back into the shed next to the Massey Ferguson.

He looked at the big machine with its huge tyres. So far, his father hadn't allowed him to drive this, but in another month, he'd be legal to drive it. *Why not give it a try now?* He knew he'd manage it fine. Dare he take it for a little drive? No one would know... Jamie ran to the house for the keys; he'd drive it up to the top of the farm track where it met the public road, turn round and come back. This would make a wicked practice run. Of course, he wouldn't drive onto the road. He mounted the steps up to the cab, started the engine, and skilfully steered it out of the shed. In just a few months, he'd be left school and driving this beast every day. No more exams and the teachers could all take a running jump!

Straining on his chain Toby barked at him as if to say, *Take me!* He probably felt left out because Ben had gone off with their master that morning. With a sigh, Jamie applied the handbrake, climbed down and untethered Toby. 'C'mon lad. Up!' The collie leapt agilely into the cab.

CHAPTER 8

Jamie clamped on headphones and plugged the lead into the radio/CD player. Immediately, a wave of classical music fed into his ears. No way! He pressed a button and twiddled the knob until he got the radio tuned into Rock FM and set off towards the track.

Despite it being nearly twenty years old, the Massey Ferguson was not only the biggest but the most valuable of the Top Thorn tractors. *I'm a good driver*, Jamie told himself proudly. Probably better than Josh, who kept reminding him he'd applied for his provisional licence. *Well, I'll be able to apply for my licence in another month.*

There was a test to pass before he'd be legal on the road, but he didn't reckon it would be very hard. In fact, he would probably sail through. It was something of a joke that sixteen-year-olds could drive these big machines on the public road, yet were unable to drive a small car until they passed the diving test at seventeen. He remembered Sally once telling the family about a year 11 boy who, one day came to school on a tractor and parked it next to the Head's Ford Fiesta. Jamie had been well impressed.

He felt quite confident that he would also pass the car drivers' test as soon as he was seventeen, as had Sally, though being a student, she couldn't afford a car of her own. Once their legs were long enough to reach the pedals, they had both learned to drive an ancient mini on the farm land. He could certainly handle a car and had occasionally moved the Land Rover and Discovery in the yard.

The two gates on the track were open, so he didn't need to stop. Passing the place where he'd found the sheep with its eye pecked out, he thought with satisfaction that the ewe was now doing well and back with the flock. His father referred to her as One-Eyed Sue. Reaching the top of the track and the spot where he waited each morning for the school bus, he hesitated and checked the road to make sure it was clear. *Shall I turn it round in the road? I can make a full sweep. It'll be easy peasy! I'll be doing this in another month, anyway.*

He crossed the cattle grid and steered the tractor out onto the road. *Wow, I shouldn't be doing this!* But his confidence took priority over rules. Carefully turning it round, whilst his eyes checked the mirrors, *yeah, clear, nowt in sight,* he positioned the vehicle to face the Top Thorn track and proceeded to drive back to the farm. *Now, that was a perfect three-point turn! Favver wouldn't have done any better.* He congratulated himself. If he could take that tractor test now, he'd definitely pass.

Swaying in his seat to the fast and lively Killers' hit '*Somebody told me*', he steered along the track and gathered a little more speed. *Perhaps I'll have a quick look at the English homework between lunch and afternoon chores.* There was a bit of geography to do as well. He mustn't forget that.

Some of the kids in his form were already talking about the year 11 prom, as if it was more important than the exams! Even Josh and Nick had mentioned it. Chronologically, the exams came first. *Yet lasses are wittering away about dresses – mad!* Perhaps it simply provided a diversion to all the exam pressure. Jamie wasn't bothered about the prom. Once those dreaded GCSE's were behind him, he would become a farmer. That was his focus. However, he knew school leavers not in apprenticeship schemes were required to do some kind of college course alongside work, until they were eighteen. *Why do people keep reminding me of this? Plenty of time to sort it out.* He planned to have a chat with Neil and get his advice.

For now, he decided to get the tractor back to the shed in case his father turned up for a late morning coffee, and he realised that his mother would be back from her shopping trip soon. It wouldn't go down very well if he was caught this far up the track with the big tractor. He was suddenly aware of a vehicle coming up behind, because headlights were reflecting in the tractor's windscreen mirror. Glancing in his door mirror, he recognised the postman's red van. *Oh shit!* He was getting closer and flashing headlights at him. What was he supposed to do? Go faster? Pull up off the track so the postman could pass? He unplugged the headphones, indicated that he was pulling in and then stopped. To his surprise, the red van stopped behind him and the postman got out, clutching a pile of letters. Jamie realised that the postman simply wanted to save himself the trouble of driving right down to the farmhouse with the mail for Top Thorn, so he jumped down and took the letters from him. Toby, recognising the postman and hoping for a biscuit or two, leapt out of the cab and pranced around, wagging his tail. The postman gave him a welcoming fuss and his treat.

Jamie whistled and called Toby to get back into the cab; 'C'mon, lad!' But Toby was outside, untethered, and relishing his freedom. He stood with all four feet rooted to the ground, his ears cocked, tongue hanging out and looked impudently at Jamie, as if to say, *You're not my master. I know more than you about this farm.*

Jamie whistled again and shouted at the collie 'c'mon, Toby!' but to no avail. Finally, he swore under his breath and climbed back into the cab. He pushed the automatic gear stick out of park and into drive. Jamie watched Toby go rocketing off and a few moments later saw him rounding up a few solitary sheep that had wandered away from the flock. He would most likely be down in the yard when Jamie got there with the tractor. Knowing that his father held strict views on dogs not being given freedom to use their own initiative, but always to work under the command of their master, he felt a tinge of annoyance. He was cross that Toby had not obeyed his command to get in the tractor cab. Effective dog handling was definitely something he wanted to learn once the GCSE's were out of the way.

He was motoring past the little copse of fir trees that grew twenty yards or so to the left of the track and as he briefly glanced in that direction, a graceful deer trotted out into the open. It looked straight at the tractor but stood poised, as still as a statue. Jamie was now moving at a moderate speed and began braking; he didn't want to hit it. A few years ago, a deer had leapt in front of the Discovery when he'd been a passenger with his mother, driving home one night. The impact killed the deer and caused a fair bit of damage to the car, the memory of which flashed through his mind.

They were very nervous creatures, so it came as a great surprise when the deer took a jump towards him from the left. Instinctively, he quickly yanked the wheel to the right and as he did so, felt the huge machine sway slightly. Trying to correct his angle, he hurriedly pulled the wheel round to the left.

The world swayed before him. As if it was trying to make up its mind, the tractor rocked and then veered sideways. He hadn't taken account that the land to the right of the track at this point receded a few feet. Too late! Jamie knew it was impossible to stop what was about to happen. In a split second, he realised that if it toppled over and turned upside down, he might die. His entire past and future flashed before him in the blink of an eye. There wasn't even time to cry out.

It happened so fast. *C..r..runch! Bang!* An earth-shattering crunch roared and reverberated around his ears. And then, *thump, crump!* And then just a whirring noise. Jamie fell to the right-hand side of the cab, his headphones yanked off, and he hit the side of his head and shoulder on the metal bulkhead. Hot rods of pain ran through his head, and everything blurred in his vision. *Am I dying?* And yet, he was still sitting in the tractor, belted in, but kind of sideways. His vision slowly cleared. For a crazy moment, he almost laughed. *I'm alive!*

The tractor had not turned over completely, but it lay on its side. *What was that whirring sound?* It was the engine. Instinctively, he stretched out a hand to turn off the ignition because he knew the wheels would be still turning, and damage could be caused to the engine. All went quiet.

Need to get out of the seat belt. It wasn't an easy task when lying on his side. Groaning and swearing aloud, he reached for the clips that would release the belt, and eventually his efforts paid off. Next, he needed to get out of the opposite door, which was now above him like a roof. Hoping that it wouldn't have jammed in the impact and somehow locked itself, he pushed and pushed. He tried to separate himself from the searing pain in his shoulder that seemed to scream in protest at every effort he made. Hot needles were piercing into his head and he felt sick. Something wet dripped onto his hand. It was sticky when he touched it and he realised it was his own blood.

Mustering all his strength, he thrust with his uninjured arm and shoulder against the door. He was strong for his age, having developed firm muscles from farm chores and sport. Taking deep breaths and steeling himself to ignore the pain, he shoved and heaved at the door. Finally, the catch released, and he slowly eased the heavy door open. Now all he had to do was climb out. Grasping the door's framework at either side, and ignoring the screaming protest of his shoulder, he swung his legs up.

Once clear of the vehicle, he collapsed to the ground, retching. Crawling away from his small pool of vomit, he attempted to stand. At first, his knees buckled. He was in shock. Then he looked back at the mighty Massey Ferguson lying on its side. Like a felled monster. The tears came flooding from his eyes and down his cheeks, mingling with his blood. He sat down on the track and sobbed like a small child. The thought of having to tell his father filled him with fear and misery. Maybe it would have been better if he'd died, as he felt sure his father would quite happily kill him when he saw what he'd done. Even if he survived these injuries and his father's wrath, he'd never be allowed to work on the farm now.

Jamie was so engrossed in his misery that he lost track of how long he sat there. Suddenly, he was aware of the sound of an engine and tyres crunching along the gravel. A car door opened and slammed, followed by light, hurrying footsteps. An arm came gently around his shoulders, and he heard his mother's anxious voice, 'Jamie, Jamie! Let me see…You're injured. Oh my God.' She knelt on the damp grass at the side of the track. 'Let me see your head. You've got a nasty cut there. It's going to need stitching. Can you stand? I'm taking you straight to A & E. You've had a bump and you might have a concussion.'

'So sorry. I'm s-sorry,' he kept repeating as she helped him slowly walk to the Discovery and settle him into the passenger seat. 'Favver … he'll kill me,' he sobbed and shivered.

Beth gave him a box of tissues and then, slotting her own seat belt in place, said, 'I'll speak to him once we get you safely into A & E.'

Jamie closed his eyes whilst his mother drove quickly but carefully through the country lanes to reach the A591, by-passing the busy streets of Kendal to reach the hospital, which lay to the east side of the town. She didn't ask him anything, and he sat quietly, holding a thick wad of tissues against the side of his forehead to stem the blood flow. *Mustn't throw up!* He concentrated hard. It was when she parked outside the A & E department that Beth made a call to her husband. Jamie held his breath in dread as they waited for Martin to pick up.

After a few moments, Beth clicked the phone off. 'He's not answering. Must be busy or somewhere with a poor signal. I'll try later. Now let's get you sorted out.'

CHAPTER 9

Beth informed the A & E receptionist that her son had sustained a bad fall and cut his head. It was best to keep matters simple, she'd told Jamie before they got into the building, and he immediately understood what she meant. They certainly didn't want any questions that might lead to trouble for the farm.

By some fluke of luck, the department was not busy. A handful of patients sat in the waiting area and were being processed methodically, which meant Jamie was little more than an hour and a half waiting and being treated. After an X-ray, a young male nurse with an elaborate arm tattoo cleaned his head wound. He joked and asked who he'd been fighting with, and then a female Asian doctor expertly stitched the wound. His shoulder was merely bruised and should feel easier after a few days. He was given a tetanus injection. On account of his head injury, they advised him to take things quietly for the next couple of days. When he walked back up the corridor to where his mother was waiting, she said, 'I've spoken to your father.'

Jamie's shoulders drooped, and he sighed. 'I can guess what he said!'

'I'm sure you can, but he also asked how you are.'

Before he could comment, the nurse appeared and repeated to his mother all that Jamie had been told. *As if I'm not capable of telling her myself*, he thought as he listened again.

Leaving the hospital building, she said, 'I expect you could do with a cuppa. I know I could.' She led him to the left of the footpath that ran along the outside and entered again through another door that opened into a bright café with soft music playing and an assortment of staff and visitors sitting at tables over beverages and snacks. Jamie sat down and waited whilst his mother went off to the counter.

Gratefully, he stirred the tea bag around in the mug until it was strong enough to drink, and unwrapped the chocolate biscuit that she'd brought him. Her phone pinged, and she opened it up quickly, murmuring, 'Your father.'

Jamie groaned inwardly. *Oh shit!*

She pored over the message, and then quickly texted back before dropping the phone into her bag. Neither spoke for a few moments. Spooning the tea bag out of her mug, she deposited it on a folded paper serviette and then looked directly at him. 'I'm sure you realise that you've been incredibly reckless and stupid.' Her voice was quiet and controlled. Jamie nodded miserably. 'How on earth you managed to over-turn such a weighty tractor really beats me. I suppose you were going too fast and maybe braked hard or something?' she went on.

He nodded. 'It were a bit like that...'

'What happened?'

He told her about the deer's sudden appearance and described his actions. 'Doesn't excuse me though, does it? I shouldna taken the Massey out...'

'No, it doesn't excuse you and I really thought you respected our rules on supervision and safety. I'm very disappointed, Jamie. Even if you had your licence, which you don't, your lack of experience doesn't make it safe for you to drive that machine out with no one supervising.'

'I know. I'm sorry.'

'Fortunately, the cab saved you from serious injury, and presumably you wore the seat belt. Both your father and I are thankful for that.' She took a deep breath. 'I'm going to tell you a story, Jamie. It's about my grandfather, whom you never knew.'

'He used to ride out on a fell pony to tend his sheep, right?'

'Yeah, and my father kept one to go up on the fells, too. That was before quad bikes took over. In fact, that was how I first learned to ride as a child. But hey, that's going off the subject. We're talking about tractors. Sadly, my grandfather turned over a tractor on some sloping land, and it was a tractor that didn't have a cab. He broke his neck and spent the rest of his life in a wheelchair.' She paused to take in Jamie's horrified reaction. 'Needless to say, my grandfather didn't do any farming after that accident.'

He couldn't trust himself to speak, so overwhelmed was he with horror, and the guilt and shame of what he'd done.

In the car, he pulled down the sun visor, and took a look at his head wound in the mirror. He knew that the nurse had shaved off some of the heavy fringe that flopped over his brow but got a shock when he saw the prominent stitches over the red line of the cut. He'd be left with a scar, and it would serve to remind him of his stupidity.

'Your hair will soon grow,' his mother told him cheerfully as she turned the ignition key and they left the hospital car park.

All too soon, she turned off the road and onto the track that led to Top Thorn. In his mind, he was wondering how badly the tractor was damaged and how much would be the cost to get it lifted onto its four wheels and repaired. Thousands, maybe. Thousands they could ill afford! Jamie was dreading having to face his father's anger.

The first vehicle they met parked on the track was the Atkinsons' Land Rover and the sight of it was a tiny relief to Jamie. Surely his father wouldn't totally explode in front of Len, his best friend? Beth parked up on a level bit of ground at one side of the track and got out to walk towards the trio of men who stood talking in front of the over-turned Massey. Cautiously, Jamie followed, his head still throbbing in pain; he'd decided it would be cowardly to remain in the car.

His father, Len and Neil Atkinson, clad in wellies, farmers' green overalls and tattered jackets, eyed him in silence.

'Well, lad, how's it ga'an?' asked his father at last.

'Ar ... reet,' he answered, steading his voice.

'Well, this en't.' Martin stabbed a finger towards the stricken tractor.

'I'm really sorry.' Jamie hung his head.

'Tha better *had* be sorry. Fer what good it'll do fer t' Massey.' He pointed to the tractor again.

Jamie sensed his father's temper was only just under control and he knew better than to say any more. A wave of nausea engulfed him, gurgling in his throat, and he rushed over to the clump of trees to vomit the tea that he'd drunk at the café.

When he straightened up and wiped his mouth with the back of his hand, Neil came over to him. 'Tha's a bit o' concussion. It won't last,' he said kindly. 'Jamie, tha not the first t' turn ower a tractor. Never think that. I did one when I were not much older than tha.' His warm brown eyes twinkled at the memory. 'The favver chased me all ower farm, shouting death threats. I had t' climb int' rafters o' one o' our barns an' hide til' he'd calmed down.' Picturing the scene, Jamie almost smiled.

'Listen, the world's not about ter end!' Neil continued. 'We're mekking a plan t' get it up without costing ter much. We've got t' telehandler at Under Clough, as yer know, and there's a guy down Levens valley that I do some work fer, who's got a big digger on caterpillars that he hires out. Reckon he'd do me a favour. I've already left him a message. Should hear back soon.' He patted Jamie gently on his good shoulder.

Jamie looked at the young man in gratitude and thought how lucky they were to have such a friend. 'Wish I had a brother like you,' he said.

Neil laughed and scratched his stubbly chin. 'But thaz got a *beautiful* sister. Brainy too!'

The up-righting of the Massey Ferguson on Sunday morning was a skilful and impressive operation by Neil with the Atkinson telehandler, and the big digger brought up from Levens on a lowloader by Neil's friend. Josh and his father had come up to watch. Although the tractor seemed to have sustained only bits of cosmetic damage and the engine started straightaway, there was an oil spillage and Martin said he would have it checked over by an engineer. Whilst they might have got off lightly, costs had been involved and Jamie carried his guilt at having unnecessarily caused them.

'Frankenstein's monster!' laughed Josh on first seeing his friend's scar. But when they were walking down to the house for sandwiches that Beth had made for everyone, he said, 'Meks yer look kinda tough. It'll be a sure hit wi' t' lasses.' Then he talked about the Saturday afternoon date that he'd enjoyed in Windermere with Sophie. She'd let him kiss her.

On Monday morning, as Jamie boarded the bus, the driver asked if he'd been in a fight with a ram. 'Summat like,' he muttered, diving into his customary seat next to a window, halfway down the bus. Physically, he felt much better, his head not nearly so painful and his shoulder just ached a bit. Sleep had helped. When Josh got on at Under Clough, he was still talking about his date with Sophie, but his words flowed over Jamie's head. He wasn't interested in hearing about Sophie's plans to do sixth form and then a Fine Arts degree.

Jamie's thoughts still mulled around the trouble he'd been in at the weekend and how fortunate that he'd not been injured worse, such as his great grandfather whom he'd never known. However, he was deeply saddened that his father no longer trusted him. Contrary to his expectations, Martin had not viciously laced into him, nor had he chased him with death threats, causing him to seek refuge in the barn rafters like Len Atkinson had done with Neil. But a cool distance had manifested between father and son. They'd avoided each other. In a way, this was worse.

'Me favver's not speaking to me,' he said to Josh. 'I'd never have thought it would be a relief to be ga'an t' school.'

'He'll get ower it,' Josh assured his unhappy friend.

'I don't want *anyone* to know how I got this.' He pointed to his scar. It was such a visible sign of his shame, of which he was reminded every time he looked in a mirror. There wasn't enough hair to comb over it. He'd be counting the days for it to grow.

'I get it, mate. Yer came off yer bike.'

'Thanks, mate.'

CHAPTER 10

At the last pick-up point, Liam Hodgson, Billy Beaty, and his small sister climbed aboard. Hodgson's mate Beaty shouted 'Yo!' to attract attention, and the younger kids in the front seats looked up.

Jamie groaned inwardly. *Those two shit-wits. What now?* Someone exclaimed, 'Wow Hodgson! Where d'yer get *that* prize?'

They all looked at Hodgson standing at the front of the bus with an ugly black eye.

'F'ckin' 'ell! Another'n. You lads!' muttered the driver.

'Bet he got it off 'is dad,' someone shouted.

'Surely not for getting library detentions?' called out Josh in mock serious tones and the bus roared with laughter.

Hodgson scowled as he strode to his seat. Even the

year 9 girls doing their make-up joined in on the banter. 'C'mon Liam, spill!'

'How many rounds yer do?' a boy yelled from the back.

'Yer shoulda seen t'other lad!' crowed Beaty, followed by snorts of disbelief from a few kids.

Jamie, not wishing to draw attention to his own disfigurement, kept one side of his face turned to the window. He certainly didn't want anyone to think he was 't'other lad!'

It was when they all left the bus outside school that Hodgson noticed Jamie's stitched gash, showing beneath his sheared off fringe. 'Been fighting as well, *farm lad*?' As he turned to walk away, Jamie heard him mutter to Billy Beaty, 'More like 'is favver socked 'im one.'

'That twat has sure got it in fer me,' Jamie sighed as he hoisted his bag onto his unbruised shoulder. 'I'd like ter get t' bottom o' it.'

'Tek nae notice,' Josh advised. 'Those two are losers.'

True to Josh's prophesy, Jamie's head injury caused sympathy. When he entered their form room for registration, several voices cried out, 'Jamie Bouthwaite! Woo hoo!' 'What've you been up to?' Girls blew him kisses.

'Nice one, mate!' shouted Nick Dixon. In answer to the barrage of questions, Jamie said he'd hit a pothole on the farm track and come off his bike. It was easier, and they seemed to accept it.

Jamie's first period was PE. On account of his injury, his mother had written a note to excuse him, and he regretted not being able to play basketball. The Crawler, (Mr Crawley), who was not only his PE teacher but also Head of year 11, made him revise his coursework in the PE office amidst overflowing boxes of lost kit and stinky trainers. He could hear the whistle shriek, boys calling out, the squeak and pounding of running feet on the gym's polished wooden floor, and longed to be out there. Near to the period end, The Crawler's lanky track-suited figure reappeared in the doorway. 'I notice that you've got some very positive predicted grades, Jamie. How come you didn't attend sixth form open evening last term?'

'No point, sir. I'm not planning to stay on after this year.'

'So you're hoping to do a course at Kendal College, or get on an apprenticeship scheme? What are your plans?'

Jamie shook his head. 'I'm needed for the farm, sir.' Even though this may no longer be the case, he thought it would close the conversation, and he was right.

'Well, you'll have to do some kind of course alongside of work until you're eighteen, so keep your options open. Meanwhile, stay focussed on the exams.' The teacher returned to the basketball match.

During lunch break, Jamie found himself flanked by Sian and Moira from his form, whilst he ate his chicken and bacon wrap. It was preferable to being taunted by those two stupid year 10 boys and having to restrain himself from retaliating. Moira tossed her long auburn tresses off her shoulder and presented him with a lemon meringue dessert that she'd bought from the counter. He smiled shyly at her and ate it. How did she know it was his favourite? As far as girls went, he decided, she was more than OK.

That evening and for several evenings to come, his father continued to treat him coolly, expecting him to spend his time at home doing homework. He'd been forbidden to go anywhere near the tractors. It was from his mother whom he learned that an engineer from R V Kelly's had been out to do an inspection on the Massey Fergusson and it was deemed to be safe. They were in the kitchen washing up whilst Martin was in the living room watching TV.

'By the way, I've something else to tell you,' she said. 'I'm joining Chrissy Atkinson with her catering business.'

'I thought you wanted to go back into teaching?' He knew she had done an odd day's supply here and there, but that it wasn't consistent and most of the work had been at a rough secondary school on the West Coast and not the primary teaching for which she was qualified and preferred.

Beth shook her head. 'I want to be here for the farm in the daytime. The advantage of working with Chrissy is that it's usually evenings and weekends. She's getting really busy and needs help at events, and especially with the accounting side that I'm good at.

And she's asked me to join the business. There's the potential to expand. She's even talking about opening a farm shop if premises came up in the village and we'd employ people. It's exciting, isn't it?'

Jamie hung his tea towel on the Aga rail and observed his mother's animated face. He didn't quite know what to say, having hoped she would find a teaching job and leave the farm work to him and his father, so he just grunted a non-committal 'Uh huh,' and went off to his room.

***

A week later, during the school lunch break, Jamie was working in the DTech department on his GCSE project, a coffee table in ash, its top carved with sheep, walls, and mountains. It was a time-consuming and painstaking project, which had started during year 10, when he'd had to write up about his idea, then order in the wood, trace the images from photographs found online and cut them out. The carvings had been put into the tabletop with a precision tool. Now it was in its final stages, and he was applying the first coat of varnish. He had been told by his DTech teacher that it would most likely earn him a top grade. But it would also be something nice to give his parents for their next wedding anniversary. After marking, Years 11 and 13 projects would be exhibited in the school hall for a week before being released to the students. Jamie was already wondering how he could get it home. With all the kids on the school bus, there wouldn't be room. Most likely, one of his parents would have to pick it up. He'd need to wrap it well and disguise it, otherwise the surprise element would be lost.

Although seniors enjoyed the privilege of being able to use the space to work on their exam projects during lunch breaks, apart from Jamie, only three others were in that day. The radio was tuned into Rock FM and the teachers were eating their lunch behind the closed door of the DTech office. Jamie was surprised when Liam Hodgson and Billy Beaty sauntered in. 'F'ckin' detention,' grumbled Hodgson. 'We en't picked our DT projects.'

'Bloody'ell! Look what cat 's brought in,' said Becca Ellis, who perched on a stool at the centre table, messily painting a ceramic lamp base.

'Losers!' called out her friend, pulling a face as if

she'd smelt something rotten.

To Jamie's annoyance, the lads dragged chairs over to sit near him. But he didn't object; he merely warned them not to disturb any dust.

'Can't be arsed to mek anything,' said Hodgson with a shrug of his shoulders.

'His mam'd never give any money fer't materials anyways,' put in Beaty. 'Nor mine would neither...'

'Shuddup Beat.' Hodgson turned to scowl at his companion.

'Huh, there's stuff yer can mek that doesn't cost much,' said Jamie.

'You suck up t' teachers, I'll bet,' growled Hodgson.

Jamie ignored the jibe. 'There's files you can look at for ideas,' he said, waving a hand towards an untidy display rack in an attempt to be helpful.

'Can't be arsed.' Hodgson sat low on the chair and stuck his long thin legs out, crossing them at the ankles. His trousers were mud encrusted in places and his shoes were in poor condition.

'Up to you,' Jamie muttered as he carefully stroked his brush around a Swaledale's curly fleece. He felt the other boy's gaze boring into the scene depicted in his design.

'School's a waste of time,' said Beaty. 'There's nowt they teach yer that's any use.' He blew his nose on a dirty lump of tissue.

'Why bother wi' all this?' Hodgson nodded towards Jamie. 'Yer'll have a job soon as yer leave.'

'Job on yer farm,' put in Beaty. 'That's summat they should teach here. Driving tractors and stuff. I'm ganna work wi' me favver when I leave.'

'Aye, working wi' pigs'll reet suit tha!' said Hodgson with a nasty snigger.

'Your favver couldna gi' tha a job. 'E can't hold down one hissel'.' Beaty gave back as good as he'd received.

Hodgson stuck out a foot, kicked the other boy in the shin, watched him wince in pain, and looked at Jamie. 'My favver used t' shear sheep, yer know. He worked on farms, all ower t' area, one time. He were well respected, one o' best. And would of…'

Jamie lifted his brush as Hodgson paused. He was interested to hear what was coming.

But at that moment Beaty leaned forward, and his

breath stank of cigarettes. ''Is favver's a boozer. Can't keep a job.'

Hodgson jumped up and got hold of the smaller lad by his collar. 'Just shut th' f'ck up Beat. I'm gitting sick o' yer mekking up stuff. F'ck off! And *you* Bouthwaite. Think yer reet better 'n us. I'm sick o' all o' yers!' Hodgson kicked over the chair.

It landed within inches of Jamie's coffee table, creating a small cloud of dust that floated in the air for a moment before descending onto the varnished top. 'Watch it, yer clumsy oaf!' he snapped, but Hodgson swore and ran out of the room.

Beaty sat in silence for a minute, watching Jamie examine his work and then he said in a low voice, 'His favver were lying in't middle o' road t'other week. Smashed.'

'Couldna care less! I'll have to redo this varnish. Bug off!' Jamie got to his feet and went to look for a bottle of turps. At that moment, one of the DT teachers came out of the office.

'Glad you're still here, Jamie,' he said, pulling on his brown lab coat and striding over to switch off the radio. 'I believe you told us you're not staying on next year. Are you interested in a carpentry and joinery apprenticeship?' He mentioned the name of a local company that specialised in designing and making bespoke furniture. 'Looking at the quality of that piece you've made for your GCSE project, I think you'd have a very good chance of getting in. The job's advertised on their website.'

Still simmering with anger at having to re-varnish the tabletop, Jamie was too stunned to speak. He had enjoyed every stage of designing and making the table, but an apprenticeship in furniture making wasn't something he'd considered. 'Er, I don't know,' he stammered, working carefully with a turps dampened rag over the affected area of his tabletop.

'Closing date for applying is about a month,' said the teacher.

At that moment, the bell for afternoon registration shrilled in their ears. Jamie put the turps back where he'd found it, grabbed his backpack and hurried out.

CHAPTER 11

On reaching home, Jamie changed out of his school clothes. The DT teacher had emailed him with the advert for the carpentry and joinery apprenticeship, which would run over three years and include college attendance. An application form was attached. After reading it through, he went outside to do his chores. If he mentioned it to his parents, they would urge him to apply. They'd be pleased if like Josh, he had an apprenticeship leading to a qualification, with job assurance upon completion. Surely whatever decision he took must be his own? So he said nothing to them at this stage.

Before feeding the dogs, he released them from their chains and let them run around the yard for a while. He often thought it was a pity that the dogs were never introduced into the house. If he had his own

124

farm, he would do things differently and give his dogs the opportunity to curl up in front of the fire in the evenings. He recalled his father's stance on the matter: '*Once you start going soft on a working dog, you end up with a house pet.*' Jamie kicked a battered football across the yard and watched the two collies joyfully hurtle after it. He didn't think his father was always right.

His thoughts came back to the issue with Liam Hodgson as he returned to the house an hour later and found Beth preparing supper. She had a laptop open on the counter next to where she was peeling potatoes. 'Mum,' he began tentatively.

'Oh there you are Jamie, could you just get a pan out and fill it up with hot water from the kettle, please?'

'Sure.' He reached into the pan cupboard. 'Er Mum … I … er want to ask you something.'

Momentarily, she raised her reading glasses to look at him. 'Is it a quick one?'

He changed his mind. 'Doesn't matter. Yer look busy.'

'Sorry Jamie. I've just got to concentrate on this.

I'm doing a presentation for the WI at Keswick tonight and I'm really at the last minute with it and need to concentrate. We've been busy here today. And late this afternoon, your father found a ewe with its uterus hanging out. We've had to strap it. You're all right aren't you? Good.'

Beth didn't stay for supper, but drove off to Keswick, leaving Jamie and his father to eat when it was ready. Jamie did the washing up alone; Martin having disappeared into the living room to catch up with the day's news on TV. Later on, when Jamie looked in on him, intending to ask if he knew Hodgson's father, he discovered him asleep and snoring in his chair. Half-past eight in the evening! Would this be him in years to come?

He went up to his room, had a go at the French homework and then played a computer game for a while. Maybe he'd have a word with his mother when she came in. His head was aching a bit.

Jamie lay on his bed, pulled the duvet up to his chin and slept for an hour. Eventually, his mother arrived home. It was nearly eleven o'clock. He heard her go into the bathroom and then straight to bed. No, the whole thing with Hodgson about farms and fathers was stupid, he told himself. It wasn't worth pursuing. He rolled over and went back to sleep.

Next morning, as the bus pulled up at Under Clough, Josh came sprinting up the track, partially buttoned shirt hanging over his trousers, open rucksack over one shoulder and tie in hand. 'Phew! Five minutes, point two seconds,' he puffed, checking his watch before flopping down into the seat next to Jamie. He delved into his rucksack to check that he had everything for the day's lessons. 'Oh shhhite!' he swore, upon discovering that his French homework was still on the kitchen table.

'Get yer mam to scan it and email it in,' suggested Jamie.

'Don't think that's a plan,' sighed Josh, threading his school tie under his shirt collar.

'Nah, mine wouldn't oblige either. Yer could copy my attempt, fer what it's worth.'

Josh snorted that it wouldn't be worth copying, and they both laughed. Then Jamie told him about the apprenticeship. He knew Josh could be trusted to keep it to himself. 'Aye, I'm sure yer could do it, nae problem and there'd most likely be job security, not just wi' them but other joinery firms. But, hey, aren't yer an outdoorsman?' He paused for a moment and then hastened to add, 'Don't let me put yer off. Gi' it a go. Anyways, yer don't have ter tek it, if they offer it yer. Sounds an opportunity ter keep yer options open.'

Jamie stared out of the window, thinking: *Fact is, I don't know what to do.* Josh took out his phone to text Sophie. The driver was playing his Queen CD too loudly for conversation anyway. He thought it was a way of keeping the kids quiet, but as most wore their headphones tuned to their Spotify play lists, they didn't hear it.

When the bus pulled up at Rose Bank Cottages, Jamie idly looked out for the two year 10s. He saw Beaty throw a cigarette down and stamp it into the ground before climbing aboard, his little sister following. But no Hodgson. 'Where's yer mate?' asked the driver, not caring either way as he momentarily reduced the volume.

'Dunno.' If Billy Beaty knew, he wasn't giving anything away.

***

Half-term week came. After a sunny start, the weather soon deteriorated into a continuous deluge, but that didn't stop the work at Top Thorn Farm. They wore waterproofs from head to toe all the time spent outside, threw them off to come into the house for a short respite, then put them back on and went out again. There was a lot of muck to be got out and spread but they couldn't do it whilst the ground was soft.

Flooding appeared in one of the lower fields, where the beck hadn't been able to cope with the sheer amount of water rushing down from the fells. As a remedy, Martin drove the John Deere with its bucket to dig out a dyke and ease the flood. Jamie went with him, climbing down from the cab to open and shut several gates on the way. He watched his father operate the bucket. There was a bit of digging that needed to be done by hand to finish off and Jamie was doing it, when suddenly he lost his footing on the bank of slippery mud. *Splash!*

Despite being clad from head to foot in waterproofs, icy cold water now got into his suit and his wellies. He climbed out of the dyke dripping, and squelched his way to the tractor, where his father sat in dry comfort. 'Yer've left shovel on t' bank.' Martin rolled down the window, laughing. 'Go back fer it, then yer might as well stay out ter open ya'at.'

Next morning, during mucking out, Jamie discovered a cow that had sustained a knee injury. He'd noticed the swelling and guessed it must have somehow slipped when going back to its stall the previous day. 'Look at number thirty-two,' he told his father.

Martin promptly brought out his 'doctor's bag' of treatments and competently dealt with it, afterwards giving the cow an injection to guard against the occurrence of infection. 'Yer need some basic vet skills ter be a farmer,' he told Jamie. 'Close observation is a good start.'

Wow! Does this mean I've done something right at last? His heart swelled with pride as he cleaned up in readiness to spend some time on schoolwork. In between the farm chores, Jamie applied himself to GCSE AQA study guides and past papers. His mother was happy that he had decided to give it his best effort. The nine GCSE's would be the very last schoolwork he would ever do! Although he'd reread the job description for the carpentry apprenticeship and been on the company's impressive website, he still did nothing about applying.

He spent the last Sunday afternoon of half-term at Under Clough with Josh and Neil, who were servicing a mower and baler. The machines were under cover in the big implement shed. 'It's as well ter git these jobs done when yer've got a quiet spot.' Neil welcomed Jamie as he selected a large spanner from the tool chest. 'Most farmers do their own basic servicing and save themselves a load o' cash.' He pointed to Josh, who had the blades loose from the mower and was poring over an instruction manual. 'Soon, he'll be bossing me what ter do.'

With the thought of saving money in maintaining Top Thorn's implements, Jamie was eager to learn what he could. He enjoyed the chat and banter with the brothers. A little wave of jealousy rippled over him when he heard that on the day that he and his father were digging out that dyke, the Atkinson brothers and their father had attended a big tractor show at Preston and appreciated a 'reet nice ham and egg tea' on the way home.

Josh seemed a bit quieter than usual. 'His lass's been away skiing in Switzerland all week. Only gets back late t'neet,' Neil told Jamie in a low voice as they stripped down the discs on the baler, ready for greasing.

After a while, Jamie asked him about the contracting work that he did on farms. 'Is this what interests yer?' Neil reached for another tool. 'Well, if tha ganna be mekking it a full-time job, yer best thing is ter find a specialism that folk need. Such as walling, fencing, hedging, putting up buildings and the like. Something that yer do all t' year round. If tha just ga'an round offering general labour, like, thaz only ga'an be mekking peanuts. Now, me, I can offer a few different specialisms. Mind, thaz got ter be fast at what tha does. If yer go baling, yer'll be paid on t' number o' bales yer mek. Same wi' shearing. Whatever tha does, thaz got to be good an' fast, an' git thasel' known, so's farmers trust yer. And yer've got t' put money int' buying yer own equipment.'

Jamie's jaw dropped. It sounded like contracting

wasn't quite as easy to get into as he'd thought. After a few moments, Neil asked, 'How yer gitting on wi' yer favver? Since yer tractor episode.'

Jamie straightened up from leaning over the machine and heaved a gloomy sigh. 'Still won't let me drive his tractors. I can do other stuff, as long as it's not driving.'

'If I know Martin, he'll come round. He's a proud man, never had it easy hissel' when he were young. From what me favver said, and don't go repeating it Jamie, Martin were clever at school and would've stayed on, but he were needed f't farm. I think he had to grow up fast and tek responsibility. Now, keep that ter thasel'. He's holding yer back a lal bit on account o' yer accident, but he'll come round.' Neil selected a different tool. 'Eh, come ower here and I'll show tha how ter strip clutch fly wheel.'

Thinking about his father, Jamie was reminded of Liam Hodgson's nasty but puzzling insults about him being a *crap farmer*, and the moment that he'd been on the brink of providing some clue as to his grievance. 'Eh Neil, yer know a lot of farmers and guys that work on farms, don't yer?

'I know a few, aye.'

'There's a lad that gets on our bus at Rose Bank Cottages. Liam Hodgson. Said his favver used t' work on farms. Seems he doesn't now.'

'What about 'im?'

Jamie hesitated. He knew he could trust Neil. 'Well, he's been a reet pain in the arse. Resents us because we live on farms. But he came out wi' some crap about *my favver.*'

'Rose Bank?' Neil scrutinised the flywheel, checking for signs of wear. 'Hodgson? There's a woman, Sharon Hodgson, as works in't King's Head at Bowness. Think she's lives theer. She's got a partner, Greg, or Gary…Hicks, that used to be a general farm worker. And I believe he were one o' fastest shearers around, once. But I dunna think he's done owt much in years. Got a drink problem and nobody'll hire 'im now. That answer yer question?'

CHAPTER 12

That evening, whilst helping his mother with the washing up, Jamie asked if the name Greg or Gary Hicks meant anything to her.

'Gregory Hicks? Some years ago we hired him for shearing, on recommendation, but he proved to be a poor timekeeper, and what he did wasn't up to scratch. In fact, I remember he made a right mess of the job, so sadly your father had to give him the heave-ho.' Beth sent the pan drawer shut with a clatter. 'Why do you ask, Jamie?'

'Oh, his lad's at our school. That's all.' *So now I know. This is why Hodge has a grudge against me!* His father must have told him he'd been unfairly sacked by Jamie's father, perhaps even blamed him for other farmers not employing him. But Gregory Hicks had neglected to give his son the true reason.

135

'Keep what I've told you to yourself, Jamie,' she said, an edge of firmness rising in her voice. 'It's water under the bridge now.'

On Tuesday morning after PE, Jamie was scrutinising his scar in the mirror over the basins in the boys' toilets. It had healed well and showed as a red line, but that would fade in time and his hair would soon grow over it. The door swung open, and he saw Billy Beaty's reflection behind him.

'Eh Bouthwaite,' the spotty faced boy said in his funny hoarse voice. 'Hodge's left now.'

'Eh?' Jamie knew Liam Hodgson hadn't been on the bus.

'Him and his mam've gone to live with his gran, like. In Kendal.'

'Aye?'

'Aye, started another school, in Kendal.'

'Yer'll miss him, eh?'

'Nah, I've got other mates,' said Beaty with an air of importance, and walked over to the urinal.

When later that week, the DT lesson came around,

Jamie was reminded about the apprenticeship offer. The teacher told him that two other students were also interested in applying. Again, he pondered on it. What if he applied and got the job? He envisioned a safe and easy future. With the money he earned, he'd save up and buy a car. Was it something that would satisfy him until the day came when his parents become too old to farm?

Jamie's sixteenth birthday finally dawned. It meant he could officially apply for his provisional tractor licence, but he needed his father's approval. Weeks ago, he'd read up everything online that he could find on the subject, finding out that a sixteen-year-old is allowed to drive a tractor on public roads to a test centre, and that the machine should be no wider than 2.45m. He was eager to start a few lessons.

Tentatively, he broached the subject with both his parents when they were eating supper. 'Yer not ready,' said Martin immediately.

'I am!' he shot back. 'Josh is taking lessons and wants to put in fer his test before the exams.'

'You're not Josh!' Martin helped himself to another spoonful of potatoes.

'But…'

'End of! Now Beth, I'm popping out fer a pint wi' Len t'neet. D'yer need any eggs?'

It was so unfair. Why didn't his mother speak up for him? Jamie burned with the injustice of his father's refusal.

***

The last day of term arrived. In the morning the ten mile fell race took place. It was an annual event involving one hundred runners, the sporty ones, across years 10, 11, 12 and 13. The headteacher, having exchanged her usual business suit for tracksuit and trainers, stood with Wilko and The Crawler on the sports field to set them off. Jamie and Josh started together. In bright sunshine, they sprinted down the school drive, across the road, up the winding lane and took the public footpath that led up onto the fells. Many of the students were wired into their personal sound systems, but Jamie preferred the sounds of nature in his ears as he ran. It was no effort for his long, muscular legs. From his experience of competing last year, he knew the advantage of gradually building up his speed rather than going all hell for leather at the start.

With a wave, he left Josh behind and grinned as he heard his friend pant and quicken his pace in an effort to catch up. But Jamie wasn't in the mood to wait. Exhilaration and a great sense of wellbeing surged, as he easily passed several runners. The view of the lake and mountains on the far shores was hazy yet stunning. A few herdwicks grazed over to his right. They'll be lambing in a week or two, he judged by their bulging bellies. *Where's the rest of the flock?* He thought of Top Thorn's seven hundred and odd sheep and how that number would multiply hugely once lambing was complete. How he looked forward to spending two whole weeks lambing!

It was windy up there on the fell, but he wasn't cold. His body was creating plenty of energy and heat. He thought he saw a sparrowhawk swooping high above, chasing after a smaller bird, and he marvelled at its wingspread. *Whoops!* He saved himself from plunging headlong and landing flat on his face after tripping on uneven ground. Better concentrate!

He was now overtaking everyone, and had

effortlessly passed the halfway rest point, at which teachers were handing out bottled water. *I can go on forever!* The thought occurred to him that he might even be in the lead, as there was no one else in sight. Then he reached a trio of sixth form boys and jogged a few yards behind them. He couldn't see anyone in front of them, but he was tiring; his calves ached, and he couldn't raise the surge of power needed to pass them. It was all he could do to keep up with their pace.

At last, they swung onto the final lap that skimmed the shoreline for a couple of miles. Daffodils fluttered in clumps close to where little waves sparkled and rippled over pebbles, making a soft sucking sound. The runners turned onto the track that ran alongside the school's playing field. In single file, they climbed over the stile and were now at the bottom end of the field. In the distance, rose the school buildings, the steep roof and chimneys silhouetted against a brilliant blue sky. Lots of students were waiting at the top of the field near to the buildings. As the first runners approached, a hearty cheer rose, followed by clapping and whistling.

Jamie came in fourth place and was proud to be the

first year 11 finisher. After taking deep breaths to recover, he drank a full bottle of water and rubbed his calf muscles. His heart was still pounding fast in his chest and sweat poured down his face. He didn't hear where Josh and his other mates were placed. Nick Dixon, who hadn't run, found him and said that around twenty runners had turned back, not completing the full ten miles.

Mr Crawley came over to him, wanting to take a photograph. 'Wait here,' he told him. Jamie wanted to change and go for lunch, but waited. Two or three minutes later the teacher reappeared with auburn-haired Moira Varty from his form. She was the first year 11 girl to finish, and from the way she was panting, had just recently come in. Their Year Head made them stand together and smile for his camera. A tall girl, Moira seemed all long legs in her brief PE shorts and singlet. Jamie was suddenly shy as their bare arms momentarily touched whilst they posed.

Later, on the bus journey home, joyful that they had two weeks with no school, the students humoured their driver and sang along with his Queen's Greatest Hits CD. Their reward was a Cadbury's chocolate creme egg as they got off at their respective stops.

'So, bro, end of term?' Sally had arrived home for the Easter holiday. Jamie grinned happily as he walked into the kitchen and dropped his bag. She came up close and stretched up to inspect his scar. 'Wow! Healed nicely. In a few months, you'll hardly tell. Mum told me all about your little happening.' As he tossed his crumpled, sweaty running kit in the direction of the washing machine, she said, 'Oh, the fell race. Who won? Not you?'

'I came in fourth overall. And fastest year 11.'

'Well run you! Actually, I was fastest girl in year 11. Who got that?'

'Moira Varty. In my form.'

'The Vartys who farm over in Langdale? She must be one of them,' chimed in their mother. 'There was a Jonathan Varty in the year above me at school. Now as I remember, there were three brothers, so one of them would be her father.'

'Mum, you know everyone!' Sally winked at Jamie.

'No idea where she lives.' Taking a canned drink from the fridge, he left the room to change out of his school clothes. His triumph in being the fastest year 11 boy was slightly diminished by Sally's revelation of having been the fastest girl. Was there nothing he could do better than her?

He spent the entire next day out with the sheep. Taking a short break, he and Sally sat together on the quad bike, companionably sharing a flask of hot chocolate that she had thought to bring. There was only one cup, but neither cared. 'I love this time of the farming year,' said Sally. 'I feel so lucky this is my home.'

Jamie agreed. 'Places are best where there's more sheep than people.' Then he said, 'Thought yer'd made a lot of new mates and might have wanted to do holiday stuff with them. What about that Milo dude yer kept on about at Christmas?'

Sally didn't answer for a moment or two and when she did, the words came tumbling out fast. 'Milo? Oh, he's history now. Or at least I am to him.'

'What? Yer saying he dumped yer?'

'This is for your ears, bro. I'm not telling the parents unless they ask. And please *don't* tell the Atkinsons.'

Jamie promised not to breathe a word. He was grateful that Sally hadn't been critical or gloating about his tractor disaster.

'Back in January,' she began, 'the friends, the guys I hang out with, including Milo, decided to have a weekend in Paris during the Easter holiday. Great idea, except that I soon realised I couldn't afford it. You know, with rent to pay for my room and I have to eat. So I dropped out. And what did Milo do? He dropped me for one of the other girls who could go. His parents were paying for him.'

'Yer could have asked our parents.'

Sally shook her head and smiled. 'Paris can wait.'

'If I call him a filthy rotter, I'm being polite,' Jamie exclaimed vehemently. 'You're far too good for him, Sal. Can't be nice having to see him all the time though, at uni.'

'I'm fine now, Jamie.' She leaned over and gave him a little hug. 'There's a lot of us. I don't have to see him every day, and anyway after this year, which has been a general medical science course, we all get split up for our majors. You could say the vets go one way and the docs the other.' She gestured with her

144

hands. 'Look that ewe over there. She's about to push it out. Let's go over.'

They walked a few yards towards the middle of the field to where a ewe crouched with her head down and her hindquarters up in the air with a big balloon protruding between her back legs. Whilst they stood observing in case the ewe needed any help, Jamie commented, 'This one's a first time lamber. It won't be twins.' Their attention was completely absorbed in the birthing for a little while, and they waited to ensure that the mother bonded with her tiny lamb. When they moved away, he said 'I know someone who'll be pleased yer don't have a boyfriend at the moment.'

'I never said I didn't have a boyfriend at the moment.'

'I know yer don't because yer'd be talking about it if yer did.'

'Ah, you think you know me.'

'I know yer don't have anyone, and *this* lad would love to take yer out.'

'And I bet this lad's Neil?'

'Aye. He really fancies yer.' They laughed together.

'Neil's a great guy,' Sally said. 'But I really don't want the complication of a boyfriend at the moment.' Her attention shifted to a ewe that lambed earlier, yet still appeared to be in labour. 'Look, Jamie. Something's not right.'

CHAPTER 13

They set off walking quickly alongside the wall, to where a ewe was writhing in agony; its newly born lamb lay forlorn a few feet away. 'What d'you think?' she demanded of Jamie.

'There's another'n in there,' he said, running his fingers along the ewe's belly.

'You could be right! Look, can you hold her still for a minute? You know how? Steady the neck and hold the back legs so I don't get kicked.' Sally, the vet in training, had taken charge of the situation. 'I'm going in there to feel what's going on.'

'You've done this before?'

'No, but I've seen our father do it.'

He squatted over the ewe, put his knee firmly on its neck rather than hold it by the horns, which was how he usually handled a sheep. But grabbing the flaying legs would better protect Sally from being kicked. It took all his strength to hold it still enough for Sally to push her gloved arm into the blooded mess at the rear end. A foul smell met his nostrils. At last, his sister gave a grunt and pulled her hand out, grasping something horrible. They both moved a short distance away from the animal, taking fresh breaths. 'Not good, Jamie,' she said, frowning. 'There's a dead lamb in there and it's disintegrating. She's exhausted herself trying to get rid of it. The poison will kill her if left. We need Dad.'

He pulled his phone out. Martin wasn't picking up. Presumably he was occupied. 'I'll go, get him. Think I know where he is.' Jamie jumped on the quad bike and flew off. Whilst his father was initially irritated to see him pushing the bike so fast, he soon grasped the urgency of the situation and climbed on the back.

The ewe was indeed in a bad way, using her remaining strength to struggle as Jamie had hold of her horns and his father held her down, whilst Sally repeatedly put her hand into the uterus and patiently removed putrefying body parts of a lamb. The appalling stink nearly made Jamie gag, and he had to look the other way. Finally, Martin produced a syringe from the capacious pocket of his overall and stuck it into the ewe's stomach. This would offer protection against infection. 'Well done lass,' he told Sally. 'A small hand is best for operations like that.'

They found a plastic sack on the bike to clear up the nasty bits. 'Keep an eye on t' yow and see how she is wi' that lamb. It's a lal 'un. Sal, go and mix a formula. In case it needs it. We'll put this pair in't trailer.' The ewe struggled to its feet and proceeded to graze.

Fine weather continued for the rest of the week. The four Bouthwaites worked from dawn 'til dusk and were counting lambs in their sleep. Jamie experienced extra satisfaction when he found the one-eyed ewe giving suck to her twins. It would be another month before the cattle could be brought out to pasture, so they still needed to be mucked out and fed each day. The midden heap was building up too. Jamie suggested to his father that he could do the job with the John Deere and its shovel. Martin refused to allow him, despite robust intervention from Sally. He said he would get round to doing it himself, 'as and when.'

'Ugh, stubborn!' Sally shook her head in exasperation. The workload at Top Thorn was unremitting, and the Easter Bank Holiday weekend passed like all the other days.

Beth and Chrissie Atkinson had catered for a village wedding and a 21st birthday within the space of seven days. Despite being exhausted, Beth seemed to enjoy the events and reported they'd made good profits.

Jamie saw Sally recording the lambing experiences for her university coursework late one night. He knew she was only here for two weeks, after which she would go to Mid Wales for a dairy placement before summer term began and the prospect of first year exams. Too tired to think about his revision, Jamie fell asleep as soon as his body dropped into bed. There was a month before the first exam. *Loads of time*.

'Yeah, I get it that there's plenty of work here,' Sally said to him when they were together outside, checking and counting lambs. 'But you really do need to ask yourself seriously whether in the long term it's enough for you. Look at Mum and Dad. Tied to the farm all year round. They never take holidays, as you well know.'

'I want to work wi' farm animals.' He stared stubbornly at the patchwork of sloping fields bordered by stone walls that lay all around them, white with sheep and new lambs.

'Me too.'

'I can't be a vet, Sal.'

'I don't expect you to. But the farm, like many others that have remained traditional, is struggling to make a profit. You must know that, Jamie.'

''Course I know. I want ter find ways of improving it. Once I'm seventeen and have me driving licence, I'll be able to contract out like Neil and work for other farms. I'll offer a specialism.' He flung a leg over the quad bike's seat and Sally climbed on behind him.

'How do you know there'll be enough contract work on other farms? From what I can see, Neil's got them pretty well covered. Mum said you've got some very good predicted exam grades, sixes and sevens. You could do sixth form, and then go on to agricultural college, or uni.'

'I'm finished wi' school. No way am I ga'an do sixth form!' He turned the throttle, stood up, and the bike surged rapidly forward. Sally clung on for dear life and swore at her brother.

***

One afternoon, Jamie went with Sally as she took up an invitation from Len Atkinson to observe the smaller lambing scale that was in progress at Under Clough with their rare breeds.

Len had a dozen each of black Welsh Mountain, Border Leicesters, white-faced woodlands, and six Portlands with their huge curling out horns, as well as four dozen native herdwicks. All except two ewes had now produced lambs. Later in the year, they would be sold for mouth-watering prices. Len had them in one of his large metal buildings, penned separately in accordance with their breed. In due course, they would be put out for grazing, but their value merited close monitoring. 'They're all tagged now,' he told them. 'A few year ago, I 'ad a white-faced woodland tup stolen.'

He was breeding a few pedigree bulls from his small cattle herd and showed them the pen, after which he led them to view his poultry and gave Sally a tray of colourful eggs. Although free range, the hens were contained within a large open area that was fenced so that they couldn't scuttle off and lay under bushes or other random places. The RSPCA's highest standard of required space per bird was applied, allowing them the freedom to scratch around and pluck their feathers. At night, they settled in the undercover nesting boxes.

Beyond this enclosure, a few ducks noisily paraded around a pond in a meadow in which four ponies grazed. When Sally jokily questioned whether Under Clough was moving into equine husbandry, the farmer told her he was boarding them for well-off families with second homes, and that a woman came up from the village to feed and muck them.

'You can't say that Len's getting left behind,' said Sally as she drove the Discovery along Under Clough's smooth track. 'They've so many money-making projects going on. Next thing you know, they'll be opening to the public, charging an entrance fee, offering tractor and pony rides with a tearoom as well.'

They both chuckled at the thought. 'Joking aside,' said Sally, slowing down as she met the road. 'Len can afford to play with his special breeds; it's a hobby. He makes so much profit with the poultry. Conversion to poultry farming was a wise move, and he did it at the right time. It's been a winner for him. And the lads are making their own way, even Josh.'

Jamie told her about the apprenticeship that his DT teacher wanted him to apply for. After a few moments' thought, she said, 'You're not entirely sure, are you?'

'I don't know, Sal. I've not said owt ter Mum and Favver because I know they'd tell me to apply.'

'Deciding on your future is important. It's got to be what's right for you.' Steering out onto the road, she said, 'You might give it a go and after a few years, realise it's not for you. Like a lad on my course, who did an electrical apprenticeship, and two years in, found he hated it and now he's studying to be a vet.'

'Did *you* always know yer wanted to be a vet?' he glanced at his sister's side profile.

'I did toy with the idea of studying music.' She gave a short laugh and accelerated for the hill. 'But animals won in the end!'

'How?'

'Oh, to cut a long story short, and put all

154

sentimental stuff aside, I felt that in terms of getting a well-paid and permanent job, I'd have more success as a vet than as a musician.'

'As simple as that?'

Sally laughed again. 'I'm sure I couldn't do it if I didn't love animals, though. And I can still play my violin when I get the urge. It's on top of my wardrobe.' Then she repeated, 'It's got to be what's right for you, bro. Nobody else.'

It's got to be what's right for you. Sally's words rang in his head.

Top Thorn's lambing was gradually winding down with only sixty-eight to go; there had been minimal losses but when it happened they all felt sad. 'In lambing, we're in the midst of life and death,' stated Martin, one morning as he, Jamie and Sally moved away from a ewe that had died before being able to birth her triplets. Sally sniffed and there were tears in her eyes when Jamie looked at her. He blinked away a tear of his own.

Two days later, they were about to remove their foul leggings and wellies in the porch, when a black Freelander drew up in the yard. It was nearly quarter to seven on the last Saturday of the Easter holidays, and they were weary, dirty and looking forward to supper. 'Oh my God! I'd forgotten,' groaned Sally, shaking back an untidy, windswept plait.

CHAPTER 14

With overalls dropped to waist level, Jamie strode out to meet Neil. 'Hi! Going somewhere?'

Neil briefly nodded to him as he got out of the driver's seat, handsome in a blue shirt and denims. Jamie noticed he'd shaved the dark stubble that usually grew around his chin. He was surprised to see Josh and Sophie sitting in the rear seat, holding hands.

Sally was still at the porch entrance and Neil took a step towards her. 'I'm so sorry, Neil,' she began. 'I had intended to phone you back, but I've been so busy that I kind of forgot. It's really lovely of you to invite me to the gig, but I can't go as I've an early train to catch in the morning and a lot to sort out tonight. I'm going to Wrexham for a dairy placement. Plus, I'm knackered...' Her lovely face bore all the signs of humble and profound apology and Neil looked hugely disappointed.

He shrugged his shoulders sadly. 'If tha' canna gan, tha' canna gan. I shouldna took it fer granted.'

Sally came out into the yard, still in her overalls, walked right up to Neil and unexpectedly gave him a little hug. Jamie thought in amusement how smelly that close encounter would have been and hoped nothing transferred onto his shirt. Though undoubtedly, the sweet aroma of the lambing pen was a familiar one to the young farm worker. 'Hey,' she said, 'Don't waste the ticket. Jamie would love to go. I'll give you the money for it.'

Neil quickly said he didn't want payment, but that Jamie was welcome to go with them if he wished. It was a gig in Kendal by a well-known local band.

'Good, that's settled then.' Sally clapped her hands at Jamie. 'Inside now. Shower and change. Be quick!' He felt annoyance at not having been asked if he'd like to go. Here she was again, treating him like a little kid! Even so, he wasn't going to refuse a gig night with his best friends. He showered and pulled on his only decent pair of jeans with a crumpled grey T-shirt he'd found trapped at the back of a drawer. Beth, who had been cooking supper and listening in on the proceedings, handed him a bun with two sausages as he came back through the kitchen around ten minutes later.

They set off for Kendal. From the back seat, Josh made a rude comment about his brother's date for the evening. Sophie giggled at first and then thought the better of it. Jamie, munching on his sausage bun, was used to banter and shot back a quote learned from Romeo and Juliet that he planned to use in the GCSE exam: *'Romeo, the love I bear thee can afford no better term than this: thou art a villain.'*

Josh responded with *'Thou claybrained guts, thou knotty pated fool, thou obscene greasy tallow catch...you bull's pizzle!'* Last term, Mrs Wilson had let the class research Shakespearean insults, something they'd all enjoyed.

Sophie giggled again but Neil, failing to recognise the humour, slowed down and dropped a gear, 'Wanna walk Josh, and us three'll see yer in Kendal?' Jamie guessed Neil was feeling sore over Sally when he switched on the stereo and eliminated the possibility of conversation.

The gig was at the Westmorland Arts Centre. Jamie shivered with his damp hair as they walked from the car park, but once they got into the venue, it was warm and buzzing with bodies. Neil took his big brother role seriously and had already warned them to stick to soft drinks and not attempt to buy alcohol. Sophie wanted to look at an exhibition of paintings on the upper floor, so Josh had little choice but to follow her. Knowing that his friend had no interest whatsoever in art, unless it was a painting of a tractor, Jamie grinned to himself.

There was nearly an hour before the band was due to play and people milled around the foyer, chatting in little groups. 'Hey! Neil Atkinson! You were in my form at school. Must be four years!' A bearded young man wearing a T-shirt bearing the slogan 'No farmers, no food, no future,' strode over to join them, followed by a striking, dark-skinned girl with a vivacious smile. Neil introduced him to Jamie as Kev, and the girl introduced herself as Alana. Both were agricultural students.

The conversation, to which Jamie listened, was

interesting. He gathered that the couple were each specialising in different areas. They exuded enthusiasm that he found infectious. Alana was involved in wildlife conservation and was researching advantages in encouraging areas of thorny scrub and water meadows. Kev saw his own future in farm management systems, but he was keen on conserving what was good from the past, including rare breeds. Their common area of agreement was in criticising the over-use of pesticides and non-organic fertilisers that ruined soil.

'You mind listening to all this?' Alana flashed a grin at Jamie.

He shook his head and smiled back shyly. ''Course he don't mind. He's a farmer, like me,' Neil answered for him.

Alana spoke passionately for a return to nature and mentioned titles of a few books she'd read. Reeling off a lot of information about the vitamin advantage to cattle being fed grass rather than grain, about which Jamie already knew, but detailing studies of fungi, trees and ecosystems, she seemed like someone more interested in research, than hands-on farming like Neil and himself.

'Some of us are doing our best,' countered Neil with a broad smile. 'But there's many farmers that can't afford the luxury.'

'It's not a luxury!' Alana declared. 'I don't know why they think it is.'

'It's tough times for the small farmer,' said Neil carefully. 'Many of 'em struggle t' make loan repayments. An' there's nothing left fer ongoing repairs n' maintenance, never mind vet bills.' Jamie swallowed and looked at the floor. He thought about the TB epidemic, not to mention the storm damage Top Thorn had recently suffered.

'That's when we need to help them find the ways and means to become fully organic. Encourage them to diversify to create another income that will pay for them to farm organically,' Kev was saying. Jamie hoped he would further expand on this and framed a couple of questions ready to ask. But Kev shifted subjects and talked about a placement he planned to do on a cattle ranch in Arkansas in the summer.

'D'yer remember t' Bell family that used ter farm

ower at Micklebarrow?' said Neil. 'Sold up two or three year ago and it were bought by some rich bod who converted it into an open farm. Well, Bells went out t' farm in North Dakota and they did say t' me I could visit any time. I'm ga'an fer a month or twa next year. It'll be very different t' how we work.' Jamie noticed that whilst Neil had moderated his Cumbrian speech at the beginning of the conversation with this couple, he was now relapsing. He was also thinking about the possibility of picking up some of Neil's work whilst he was away next year. *What an opportunity!*

'Huge farms over there. Factory farming!' said Alana with a snort.

'Not necessarily,' said Kev. 'Go for it, Neil. Be a good experience.'

'Talking of experience,' Alana began on another tack, 'I did a work placement last year with kids from schools in Liverpool. We were introducing them to land based skills. These were kids who didn't know what happens on farms or in the country. In fact, many hadn't set foot beyond their urban environments. Others were bored with school and often in trouble.'

'What did you have them doing?' asked Jamie, glad to get a word into the conversation. For some reason, he thought of Liam Hodgson.

'Well, in the beginning we got them thinking about how in past centuries people depended on what they could grow and rear to feed themselves. We moved on to looking at trees, had them measuring girths, working out ages of them, learning about our country's forestation and deforestation, grasses and soils. And *lots* more. It was a successful project and really engaged most of the kids.' Alana's enthusiasm for the project was evident.

Having looked at the art exhibition, Josh and Sophie reappeared and the four of them joined the queue to get into the gig. Kev and Alana filtered away into the crowd, but in his mind, Jamie was still replaying some of the conversation and relevance to Top Thorn.

It was a standing event in the venue and fairly packed. Jamie started off standing with Josh and Sophie as they waited for the band. He noticed Josh's arm around Sophie's waist, drawing her close, and it became evident that he was spare, so he moved back to stand with Neil.

'The kid brother's reet loved up at t' moment. Doing better than me,' Neil said with a rueful laugh. Knowing that there was one girl Neil fancied and that she was proving to be an elusive one, Jamie said nothing. He went with him to the bar where they bought three bottles of coke, two of which were handed to Josh and Sophie, and there was a beer for Neil.

Undoubtedly, Sophie was pretty, with her elfin features and silky dark hair. In a clingy white top, and shiny black pants that hugged her slender figure like a second skin, she looked so much older out of her school uniform. No wonder Josh was obsessed. All the same, Josh was his best friend. They were closer than brothers. No, it wasn't jealousy he was feeling, nor was he resentful of Sophie. It was more a gnawing sadness for the inevitable change in their friendship now that they were growing up. Each of them would soon be taking separate directions once school was over.

For the first time, he wondered when he would

have a girlfriend. In fact, he wasn't sure if he wanted one just now, although many lads of his age did. Momentarily, he thought of attractive girls at school, Grace and Kate in his maths and IT sets, and Moira in his registration group. Moira, with her beautiful auburn hair, who'd bought him the slice of lemon meringue pie and had posed with him on the photograph after the fell race. She'd been in his registration group since year 7, and what did he know about her? Nothing. Maybe, he'd try to change that soon.

They settled to enjoy the band and Jamie didn't think about anything, other than the powerful vocals from the bald-headed lead singer and the amazing guitar riffs, great keyboarding and drumming that assaulted his ears for the next couple of hours. The audience was in its element, stamping and shrieking at the end of each number. After a brief break, during which there was a big surge towards the bar, the band again took to the stage. Jamie had bought cokes for himself and Neil. He hadn't seen Josh and Sophie during the break but caught sight of the back of Josh's curly top a few rows in front, once the band had got going again.

The first number was a creditable cover of The Animals' classic, 'The House of the Rising Sun' which went on for over ten minutes, and the lead singer's face dripped with sweat. Jamie put his drink down on a table and enthusiastically clapped. They followed this with Chuck Berry's 'Roll Over Beethoven,' and Steppenwolf's 'Born to Be Wild', obviously included to please the senior element. He'd noticed people who looked as old as his parents or even older. It'll be all oldies now, he thought resignedly, as he moved towards where he'd put his glass down. The singer then proved him wrong, by introducing some of the band's own very diverse and up-to-date compositions.

He took a swig of his coke and swallowed. It tasted different. *Must have picked up the wrong glass.* Perhaps this was somebody's vodka and coke? Or rum and coke? He didn't know the difference. After taking another sip, he guiltily put it back on the same table.

Wondering how Josh and Sophie were enjoying the music, Jamie cast his eyes around, and this time didn't see them. He was about to re-join Neil, but saw that he was with a red-headed girl and an older couple. There was another short break, in which he glanced around, observing that everyone seemed to be with someone. There were so many people in here. His forehead felt clammy and his armpits were wet as if he'd been running. Edging his way around the room, he looked again for his friends. He couldn't see them and needing to make a toilet visit, slipped out of the venue area and into the corridor that led down to the foyer. Whether it was the change of atmosphere, he didn't know, but a slight dizziness came over him.

Out of the people hovering about the foyer, he spotted Josh near to the toilets, hands in pockets. He waved to him before going into the Men's. There was someone in a cubicle, noisily throwing up. When he came out, Josh approached him, his face agitated.

'Eh, whatssup, mate?' Jamie heard his own voice sounding slurred.

'It's Sophie. Came over funny, like, dizzy and wanting to puke. Think she's ill.' Josh nodded towards the Ladies' toilets.

'She's in there?'

'Aye. I can hardly go in there and see if she's reet, can I?'

'But yer can ask ssomeone. L…Look, here's a woman coming. I bet sshe's ga'an there.' Jamie swayed slightly as his head took a spin and he looked for somewhere to sit.

The woman was indeed about to enter the Ladies' room when Josh stopped her. A minute later, she came out leading a trembling and white-faced Sophie. Josh guided her to a seat. 'Feel terrible,' she moaned. 'Everything's swaying. Don't know what it is.' She began to retch.

'Can yer fetch me brother?' Josh said frantically to Jamie. 'She'll have to be taken home.'

Jamie attempted to stand and suddenly his head whirled, and his vision swam. 'I…er don't feel so great mesel'.' Nausea engulfed him, and he stumbled towards the Men's, just making it in time to vomit into a toilet. He swilled cold water in his mouth and spat it out.

When he came out, still unsteady on his feet, Josh was texting. 'I'm trying ter get hold o' Neil. Happen

I'll have ter look fer 'im. Just stay here wi' Sophie, can yer?'

Jamie remembered very little about the next hour. He heard Neil say, 'It looks like the two o' yers been spiked.' He asked what drinks they'd had, and if they'd had any alcohol. Both had only drunk cokes and a Fanta.

They were in the car. He vaguely remembered getting into it, and being aware that Sophie had needed to be carried. At least he could walk. 'I'm tekking you t' hospital. Git yer both checked,' Neil said.

Jamie tried to protest. *Not again!*

'We're not tekking any risk. I'll phone yer parents when we git there, and Josh, you can phone Sophie's.'

CHAPTER 15

Jamie vomited at the roadside on the way to the hospital. Neil told him that whatever had been put in the drinks was like strong alcohol. He wondered if this was how you felt when you were drunk. It didn't seem a lot of fun. He was dizzy and seeing double. Josh had to help him get back into the car.

Somehow, Neil and Josh got their two casualties into the hospital and found them all seats in the A & E department. Jamie lost track of the time they waited. The department was short staffed and busy, as it always was on a Saturday night. Patients and their companions sitting in the rows of chairs occupied boredom by staring at their phones. Jamie closed his eyes. It was better that way. He was conscious of Neil and Josh talking to each other and then to some other people whose voices he didn't recognise. Later, he would learn that Sophie's parents had taken charge of her, and that Neil had spoken to his parents, assuring them he would bring Jamie home once the hospital had examined him.

For now, he thought he was still at the gig; he could hear and feel the thump of the music and see the lights flashing silvery, green and purple, and sensed the movement of applauding, shrieking people around him. He didn't remember a blood sample being taken, but emerged slightly from his hallucinatory state, whilst being guided out onto the hospital car park by Neil and Josh. Why were his knees so wobbly?

'Fortunately, yer didn't drink much o' it. Yer'll feel much better in't morning. Same wi' Sophie. It appears there were a few others got spiked as well, some a lot worse,' Neil told him. 'Hospital recommend yer report it t' police, as spiking is a criminal offence.'

Spiking. Jamie remembered covering the subject at school in those boring PHSE lessons, but had never imagined it would happen to him. He closed his eyes as Neil drove home.

Too soon, the Freelander rumbled into the yard at Top Thorn. Jamie would have preferred to sleep it off in the car; so safe and comfortable it felt, and Neil would look after him. The lights were on as he clambered out and tried to walk unaided to the kitchen porch. Neil went in with him while Josh stayed in the car.

His parents, both wearing serious expressions on their faces, awaited him. As Jamie flopped into the nearest chair, his father burst out: 'I'd have thought that wi' someone responsible like Neil looking after tha t'neet, tha'd have managed ter stay outta trouble!'

'Shhush!' Beth shot her husband a reproachful look.

'Wi' t' greatest respect, Martin,' said Neil, smiling and raising a hand, 'The kids did nowt wrong at all, and weren't t' only ones ter git spiked t'neet. They were on soft drinks, and both had t' sense ter leave it, when it didn't taste reet.'

'It's a criminal offence and we'll report it,' said Beth. 'Thanks so much, Neil, for looking after Jamie.'

'His symptoms are like a hangover, but he should feel more hissel' tomorrow.' Neil moved towards the door. 'He's had a blood sample tekken, so yer might hear back in a few days from t' hospital what were in t' spike.'

Jamie dropped into bed full dressed, closed his eyes and drifted into a deep sleep. He didn't see Sally before she left for the station very early the next morning. Upon waking up and feeling a clearer head, he switched on his phone and found a message.

Hi bro, I'm on the train. Really sorry to hear you and Sophie ended up getting spiked last night and hope you're feeling better now. It's a crime - do report it to the police. I looked in on you before I left, but you were asleep and didn't want to disturb you.

On my way to the diary placement and hope the other student working with me will be half as good as you've been during lambing. You're great with sheep! Good luck with the exams and keep up the revision. xxx S

He took a shower, cleaned his teeth, pulled on some clothes and ran downstairs. There was one thing on his mind and that was food!

'You just can't imagine the mentality of these criminals. What on earth do they get out of it?' exclaimed Beth, whilst Jamie tucked into scrambled eggs and toast.

Martin still appeared somewhat disgusted with him. *I'm being judged unfairly. The spiking could have happened to anyone – and it wasn't just me that got it. Really! What's up wi' Favver?* Jamie was at a loss to understand.

CHAPTER 16

With his future as yet undecided, Jamie stepped into his last term at Mereside Academy. The first half passed swiftly. All lessons were revision sessions for year 11. Those who were planning to stay on for sixth form had a taster day. Jamie's form tutor tried to persuade him to participate, but he firmly refused. If it hadn't been for extra sessions of sport: cricket and tennis, as well as one of the hotels offering the school an occasional booking of its swimming pool, he would have found these weeks very tedious. Instead, he enjoyed taking full advantage of all the sport.

There was a visit to the agricultural college near Preston, and a small group of students went down by train. It turned out to be an interesting and informative day with taster sessions and lectures. Jamie liked what he saw and heard. In fact, for him, it was a revelation.

He began seriously thinking about the possibility of taking a few selected BTEC level 3 courses, equivalent to A-levels, offered by the agricultural college. Nick Dixon was also interested. It would enable them to study for a qualification and even work part time, with the opportunity to fast track onto a foundation or honours degree in a variety of subjects, with work placements, if they wished. For Jamie, that subject would be agriculture.

Three of the others, including Moira Varty, intended to do a full degree in agriculture, which might or might not be at this college. But first, they would stay on at school for A-levels. 'I milk at our farm with my dad and help with the sheep,' Moira said as they trooped out of the first lecture. 'I know he'd give me a job straightaway, but I'm not in a rush. I want to go into farming with a degree.'

Jamie glanced respectfully at Moira and sat next to her in one of the lectures. He became acutely conscious of her breathing and faint perfume. When her knee accidentally brushed his leg, as she chuckled at a remark made by the lecturer, an electric current shot through his skin. His blood hummed. He needed to drag his attention back to the lecture several times. Nick on his other side, talked non-stop before and after the lecture.

'There's a lot to offer here,' said Jamie as they all sat around a table in one of the college's coffee bars. He'd been impressed that the college actually kept their own livestock and had workshops full of agricultural machinery, as well as the range of vocational courses on offer. And he liked the sports facilities.

'I kinda like the idea of living in halls here and getting a job whilst studying part-time. I can't *wait* ter leave home.' Nick flipped randomly through a pile of course leaflets that he'd picked up.

Jamie realised that study at this college, even part-time, would most likely involve having to leave home and be resident in halls, most of the week. Would that bother him? Maybe it wouldn't be such a bad thing. He mulled it all over in his mind during the train journey home, sitting next to the chattering Nick, all the while hearing snatches of musical laughter from Moira, distinctive from the others.

Half-term arrived two weeks after the college visit.

It was the last day at school for year 11 and the start of study leave. Even though many of them were destined to come back for the collegial sixth form, it symbolised the end of an era. From past experience, the senior leadership team was well prepared for high spirits and mischief, so the fire alarm had been switched off and extinguishers temporarily removed.

There had been a long assembly for Jamie's year group, during which they viewed a film that started off with a formal clip of them taken in year 7 and then went on to feature the chief events of their final year. He blushed when a clip of himself finishing the fell race, followed by another clip of him posing with Moira, came onto the screen. What a stupid, forced grin on his face! In contrast, Moira was smiling sweetly. Fleetingly, he remembered their arms touching and then sitting next to her during that lecture at the agricultural college. A guffaw of laughter erupted from Josh and some of his mates who were sitting near him, but there were also good humoured cheers. Probably for Moira, he thought. The assembly was followed by a photo session at the front of the main entrance.

By morning break, no longer restrained, exuberance and high spirits burst forth. Some year 11 form groups were dancing congas around the yard, boys with trousers rolled up to their knees and girls with skirts rolled much higher. And then there was the shirt signing ritual. One boy had discarded his shirt because there was no more room for signatures and was now offering his bare chest and back. Jamie and Josh, with Sophie between them, had arms draped around each other's shoulders; all three wore their ties around their heads like bandannas and they strutted about the yard singing 'We are the Champions!' Due to their bus driver's obsession with Queen, the boys knew all the words.

At lunch time there was a small queue at the library to return books. Jamie proudly presented 'A History of Tractors' that had finally come to light under his bed a few days ago, when he moved it to retrieve some coins that had dropped out of his trouser pocket. He held out his hand in expectation of the £5 contribution Mr Black had taken off him. But the librarian merely said thanks, wished him good luck for the exams and scanned the book back onto the computer.

During the afternoon, students went around the classrooms saying goodbye to their favourite teachers. Many gave them thank you cards and small gifts. Even Jamie felt a little emotional as he left his form base for the very last time. Five years, where had they gone?

'Bye Jamie!' At the end of the school drive, he saw Moira waving cheerily, before climbing into the passenger seat of a silver-grey Range Rover. He waved back and was about to call out to her but she'd already shut the door and the engine was running.

There was a week before the first exam. Jamie settled into a routine of working mornings on the farm, and in the afternoons a couple of hours were spent on revision. His tractor licence continued to be a no-go area, and it was frustrating.

He was thinking seriously about the possibility of going to college, but had also downloaded the apprenticeship application form and started to fill it in. The closing date was within three days. If he worked locally, he could still help out on the farm as much as he did now, but if he went away to college, he could only do this at weekends and vacations. He had a photograph of his exam project to attach to the application. Sophie, who was arty, had declared that his table was the best of all the DT projects in their year, and that he had artistic talent. He tried to imagine himself in a joinery workshop, selecting woods, sawing and modelling it into stylish tables, cabinets and curved back chairs. Then he tried to imagine himself coming out of the college lecture theatre, researching agricultural systems and travelling to diverse placements.

The two paths into his future ran side by side in his mind. Which one should he take?

One evening, his parents went out to a concert at Ulverston, featuring some famous pianist, of whom Jamie had never heard. It was a rare treat and Beth had got the tickets months ago. Martin protested, his excuse being that there was a cow that might or might not be prematurely carving. As she was sometimes able to do, Beth overruled him.

Martin stood by the kitchen door, unusually smart in grey trousers, a crisp white shirt and fine tweed jacket; he prodded a finger at Jamie. 'If anything's happening, text me. We'll come reet back.'

The late spring day had been warm as summer, and now shimmering rays of evening sunshine fell across the yard. At a loose end, Jamie kicked the football around with the dogs for a while. Later, he planned to settle down to his revision, which was by now becoming boring. Perhaps this was because he'd already revised so well. After re-attaching the dogs to their chains, he looked in on the cow that his father had mentioned. Any day now, the herd, or what was left of it following the ravages of TB, would be put out to pasture as the ground was firming up.

Martin had put the black cow in the large stall at the end of the barn nearest the door and she was lying down. Jamie carefully walked over to take a good look at the huge bulge. The vulva was swollen, but that was expected. If she was going to calf later tonight, lying on her side was the best position for her to be in. He'd assisted his father with calving last year on a couple of occasions, but the cows usually did it themselves with no intervention necessary. In any case, this cow wasn't due for another month. He stayed a few minutes, topping up the drinking water and then went outside again.

Ping! There was a text message on his phone from Josh. *Hey mate, fancy testing on revision?*

Jamie needed no persuasion. An hour testing each other would be better than two hours testing himself. He locked up and hopped on his bike.

After a chat on farming matters with Neil and Len Atkinson, who were in the yard lifting a gate onto the trailer, he went into the house to look for Josh. He found his friend sprawled full length on his bed, in tartan boxer shorts and a lurid T-shirt, with his laptop open.

'What yer looking at?' Jamie kicked a pair of trainers out of his way and glanced at the screen. It was R V Kelly's website. The page was covered with photographs of tractors, various agricultural implements, awards that the company had won, and groups of grinning workers.

'They want me ter start ASP. Day after last exam.'

'Thought you had ter get good grades?'

'Aye, they seem happy wi' what I'm predicted.'

'Not a lot to worry about, then?'

'Mebbe not, but if I did badly, they'd have ter

know. I'll also be on six months' probation.' He added that he was expected to go away for training blocks in college at Preston, starting in September, and that as an apprentice he'd have to spend most of what he earned on buying his own tools. Reaching over to the chair next to his bed, he grabbed a school file. 'Let's test each other.'

They began with biology, the first scheduled exam, taking it in turns to ask and answer questions. Around an hour later, Josh slammed shut the geography file and observed, 'Considering we had such a crap teacher this year, I reckon *you've* got that one nailed, mate!' Then he said, 'I went ter Sophie's yesterday ter revise French.'

'What? French is a waste of time. But I thought yer said her parents didn't want yer seeing her, at least 'til after the exams.'

'They were out at work,' Josh said with a smirk.

Jamie drew in his breath. 'I'll bet yer didn't get much French done.' When Josh smirked again, he said. 'Yer dirty tyke!' He made a move to grab his friend by the neck, but Josh was quicker and held him in one of the wrestling holds they'd practised, similar to the grasp that Jamie had used on Liam Hodgson on the library stairs. The difference this time was that the mood was jocular with Josh laughing as he accused Jamie of being jealous. Jamie wriggled and Josh lost his hold on his neck and they both rolled onto the floor, practising wrestling hypes and twists. Eventually, Jamie sat on top, trying not to laugh. 'Well, did yer?'

'Get much French done? Aye, a lal bit.'

'Only a bit?'

'As *you* rightly observed, French is a waste of time. Anyway, yer've a dirty mind, Bouthwaite.'

They got to their feet, slapped each other on the back and ran downstairs to raid the kitchen for drinks and snacks, just as Len and Neil arrived. 'Done much revision lads?' asked Len. This was met by guffaws of laughter and Jamie asked Neil if he'd spent much time on French revision at which Neil answered it was one that he'd failed. This caused more hilarity between the sixteen-year-olds.

Len opened the big fridge and produced cans of beer. Winking at the two boys, he said through the side of his mouth, 'No need t' tell yer mams, eh lads.'

Jamie grinned as he cracked open his can, quite sure that his own father would never have offered him beer.

He had stayed a little longer than he expected. *Better get back to check on that cow.*

CHAPTER 17

Whilst cycling back to Top Thorn in the chilly dusk, the wind pulling at his hair, Jamie was acutely aware of all the sounds of nature, an owl's low distinctive hoot, tiny scuffling sounds of mice and insects in the grass that grew at the roadside and the distant bleating of sheep and lambs. As he recalled the banter with Josh, he thought about Moira, working on her father's farm and doing exam revision. Perhaps he'd pluck up courage for a chat when they were in school for their exams.

After putting his bike away, he slipped into his wellies and overall and went out to the barn. The familiar smells of urine and dung on straw, the heavy breathing of sleeping cattle and the damp sweaty warmth of their bodies met him. The black cow was lying on her side heaving slightly, tail up and one back leg in the air. Jamie had seen them in this position many times and knew to stand clear and jump back if necessary in case a cow got up and charged. *She's not doing much.* He carefully walked over, knelt down and ran his hands along the bulge, just he'd seen his father do.

Just as he was on the verge of getting up and leaving her to it, the cow grunted and began heaving more violently. He looked under the raised leg and saw, for a few seconds what looked like a whitish, grey ball, before it closed up. 'She's presenting!' he said aloud.

He dragged over a rickety stool and must have sat for half an hour, occupied with his own thoughts about his future and the decisions pressing upon him, before another contraction came, and the same grey ball appeared before quickly disappearing again. His father sometimes put on a full-length sleeve glove and inserted his arm inside to feel what was going on. He thought about Sally, who would do this many times in her career as a vet, and remembered his father saying farmers needed basic veterinary skills. Jamie was unsure at what stage he should put his hand in, if at all, so he just watched. Last year, when he'd helped his father with a calving, it had gone on like this for ages. In fact, they'd gone indoors and drunk tea whilst they waited. He pulled out his phone to check the time. It was 9.33. When would his parents get back? He'd no idea of their concert's duration.

Twenty minutes passed. He looked around to check what equipment was available on the shelves near the door. There was a box of rubber gloves, jars of lubricant, ropes, and chains. The cow seemed quiet enough. Should he make an internal inspection?

He remembered watching as his father began easing first his fingers, then hand and eventually most of his arm was inside the cow's uterus. How quick Martin had been in making the examination. His words came to him: 'Can feel the head … though it's backward facing … and the fetlocks. It's small enough. Should come out.'

Jamie reached for a full sleeve glove and the lubricant, and was rolling up the sleeve of his overall, when unexpectedly the cow lumbered to her feet, lurched over to the water trough and began drinking noisily.

OK, I might as well go in and get a drink myself.
He laughed aloud and made his way back to the house. Sitting in the warm kitchen, clasping a mug of hot chocolate, his mind was drawn again to the two career choices open to him. He envied Josh, whose future seemed so clear. Carpenter or farmer? What if he got the apprenticeship, and there was no certainty of that, because lots of kids were looking for apprenticeships, and his application would be a late one? But - if he did secure it, he'd start earning straightaway. If he went to agricultural college, it might be years before he started earning and would his father even want him for the farm?

He reached for his phone to check the time, even though there was a clock on the wall. 10:41. *Dong, dong, plop!* His phone began to ring out. *Mum. What does she want?* Her voice was breaking up due to poor network coverage.

A few seconds later, the landline phone rang. 'There's been an accident on the main road and we're being diverted, so it's taking us longer to get home,' his mother told him. 'Is everything all right, Jamie? Your father's a bit concerned about that cow that

191

might be early calving.' He heard some muffled speech from his father, who was obviously driving.

'Fine,' he answered. 'Nowt ter worry about.' A warm glow of confidence spread from his heart and into his entire being.

Once again, he got into his wellies and strode out to the barn, which was shrouded in full darkness now. A hoarse mooing met his ears. He flicked on the lights. Matters had progressed. Still on her feet, the black cow was swaying from side to side. Cautiously yet confidently, he moved forward; he knew a cow might suddenly kick out and despite wearing steel toe capped wellies, you could still suffer injury by getting your foot stamped on.

The tail was up and he saw the cow's vulva had opened up, revealing something. *Is she about to calf now?* The cow continued to rock to and fro, taking a few steps as she grunted. In that instant, the memory came back to him of an occasion last year when he'd helped his father with an indoor calving. Sadly, that calf had turned out stillborn. *Please let this one be alive.*

She'd deliver easier on her side, he thought, *but I*

won't be able to get her down safely, so it'll have to be this way. He grabbed the rope from the shelf, made a loop and threw it over the cow's neck, then attached the loose end to an iron hook on the wall. This would stop her from walking around. At the next contraction, what looked like a little hoof appeared at the cow's rear end. He remembered Martin getting hold of it with one hand and pushing his other hand, then arm, all the way into the uterus to pull out another hoof.

Jamie brought over the calving chains and dropped them in the straw. These would be needed at some stage. Last year, he had actually helped his father attach the chains. The memory played before him like a YouTube video. *Gloves* – he needed those. He sat on the rickety stool and waited patiently. The cow could probably do it herself. Another half hour passed. That little hoof was hanging out now.

He jumped up and grasped it. At the next contraction, another hoof tried to make its way out. Instinctively, he worked his right hand around and inside the opening until he could get a firm hold on it. Now he had two hooves out. No chance was it going back in. He bent down and picked up the chains, attaching one loop end around each hoof. A length of rope provided an extension to the chains. His father's words came to him: *'Yer work with the contractions. That's the way yer do it. Here Jamie, tek the rope and when she strains, pull, but only then. Tek a rest in between. Quick now, get hold!'*

Jamie held the rope, waited and sure enough the cow began to strain. He pulled steadily and saw the whole of the calf's head emerge, sticky and slimy. He held his breath and tried to remember what they'd done next. *'Won't be long now,'* his father had said. When it was half way out, Martin had removed the chains, and they'd done the rest by hand. But Jamie was alone now, and if something went wrong, he might get into further trouble with his father … *No mustn't think like that!*

Another contraction from the cow and more of the calf's slimy body emerged. Quickly, he dropped the rope and struggled to free the two front feet from the chains. Then, he gasped and fell back as the whole body came out followed by a gush of red fluid. A small bull calf dropped onto the straw. It didn't move.

But the cow came round to sniff at it when Jamie

untethered her neck. She gave it one lick, and then another. Jamie willed the calf to move. 'Come on,' he whispered. *Move!*

'Well done lad!' Jamie got to his feet and turned round in shock. His father stood in the doorway, an overall hastily pulled on over his best trousers and shirt.

'We need ter git it breathing quickly.' Martin knelt and pushed his fingers into the calf's nostrils to clear them of fluid. Then he produced a long, clean strand of straw and tickled its nose. 'Git some water, Jamie and trickle it into the ears. Should mek it shake its head.' This did the trick. The calf started to show signs of life and took its first breaths. 'Let muvver tek ower now. It's a lal 'un but I'm sure it'll live.'

Jamie stood back with his father and watched with great satisfaction as the calf found its way to its mother's milk. They raked away the soiled straw and spread some fresh straw all around the pair. Finally, Martin stuck a syringe into the cow's stomach to help with the expulsion of the afterbirth. With cow and calf happy, they trudged back to the house. Jamie smiled proudly. His heart was bursting with emotion. This must surely be one of the best moments farming could offer.

'It's time we had a proper talk about your future,' said Martin, thrusting an arm around Jamie's shoulders. The son was now as tall as his father, something neither of them had noticed before, as they walked towards the porch. 'Fer a start, you'll have yer tractor licence. The form's filled in. Just needs yer signature.'

About time too! Jamie caught his breath but didn't dare comment as he followed him into the porch and threw off his soiled overalls. Beth had already gone to bed.

'Yer've finished school, or yer will have done once yer exams are over. And I get it that yer don't want ter stay on fer sixth form, so I'm not about to bring that up. D'yer want a brew?' Martin flicked the switch on the kettle.

Jamie shook his head. He was still on an emotional high from his first solo calving experience. The cow and her calf had been safe in his care. It was something that he'd done well.

'Did yer enjoy t' concert?' He didn't particularly

care whether or not his father had enjoyed his evening out and didn't know why he asked. It seemed of little significance.

'We did that! And it got me t' thinking a lot o' things, some that I've not thought much about in years.'

'What?'

'Oh, things,' he said evasively, pouring milk into his tea and reaching for the biscuit tin. He dunked a digestive into his tea. 'But first, I want ter say that yer mum and me, want yer to have your own choice about what yer do next. No need fer yer to worry about the farm. Yer mum and me are exploring some fresh ideas ter generate more income. We've been busy. And if it's here that yer want to work, well, yer can do, alongside some trade that yer can learn at college.'

He fixed Jamie with his keen blue eyes. 'Yer can rest assured, Top Thorn will always be here for yer. I think, whatever yer do first, yer might even want to go out to Australia and work, and yer'd have my blessing if that's what yer want, it's a big world out there, but…' To Jamie's surprise, his father's voice quavered and he sniffed. 'Oh sod it, I'm nae good at this emotional stuff.' He sniffed again. 'What I mean is yer've got the heart fer Top Thorn. Am I reet?'

Jamie nodded and sat down opposite his father.

'All along,' Martin continued, 'I've never wanted ter force yer into farming. I wanted yer ter have the choice that I didn't. I were academic at school and could've gone on ter sixth form. I were good at music and wanted ter go further wi' it. Me and another lad at one time were going ter Keswick fer classical piano lessons. And, I'd just joined some lads in a rock group. I were t' keyboard player.'

Unable to visualise his father in a band, playing a gig such as he'd attended in Kendal, Jamie smiled, despite the nasty memory of being spiked. But Martin went on, 'Me favver died suddenly an' I had ter run t' farm. I were just sixteen an' there were no one else. The farm had a mortgage on it then, so me mother would've had ter sell. We'd have lost everything. I didn't want ter be a farmer but it were forced on me. In a moment of despair, I told me mother ter sell t' piano. And she did. That were that.' He laughed softly and inspected his calloused hands. 'I've not played in all these years.'

This revelation came as a surprise to Jamie; he'd always assumed that the manual, day-to-day routines of the farm had been his father's choice. He'd never imagined his father doing anything else other than farming, and wondered why he'd kept quiet about his musical talent. 'You could get another piano or a keyboard and play as a hobby?'

'Mebbe I will. But yer know what? I grew ter love farming. Oh, I've been happy,' Martin said, leaning forward across the table. 'Yer mother and you two kids made it all worthwhile…But the gist of this story is I want yer ter mek yer own choice and not feel pushed either way.'

'I want to farm.' Jamie surprised himself by adding, 'Eventually.'

'Ah, you'd like to get a trade and work away first?'

Jamie shook his head. 'I don't wanna be a joiner or plumber. It's farming that I wanna do. But - I used ter think farming were just about rearing stock and driving tractors.' He coloured slightly as he remembered his tractor mishandling catastrophe. 'There's so much more ter farming, isn't there? And I want ter learn as much as I can. I want ter do college first and study agriculture.' It was a relief to have reached and voiced his decision. He realised he'd made it that evening during the calving. A weight lifted from his shoulders. 'Yer know I had that visit t' college at Preston?'

Martin smiled broadly and selected a custard cream from the tin. 'I know yer looked at courses, Jamie. 'Yer may not even need A levels for some, but if yer do, it's only two years ter get 'em. Two years might seem a long time to yer now, but it isn't.'

Again, Jamie shook his head. 'Thing is, I can start in September, I'd like ter try for a place ter study BTEC agricultural courses. I could still do weekends here. And then, there's the option ter fast track onto a degree, if I want.' He smiled, as he visualised opportunities for research, and learning how make the farm economically sound, widen out in front of him.

'Sounds like a plan,' said his father nodding in approval and slapping a hand down on the table. 'Now, here's a question for yer. If you were ter tek ower the farm now, what decisions would yer mek first?

Jamie thought for a few moments and then said

slowly, 'Well, first I'd be thinking about replacing the cattle we've lost and getting another bull, and how ter go about it? I mean, like, we've had a bad experience wi' TB.'

'Exactly!' Martin's face lit up. 'You think like me. I'd want ter be careful where I buy from. Now, Len will have an Aberdeen Angus ready in about six months. He'll be expensive, but he'll be a good un. However, it'll be a family decision, not just me, on whether we increase the herd or finish wi' it.'

They discussed ideas concerning the stock and then Martin said, 'Once yer exams are out o' t' way, we'll talk more.' As Jamie stood up with a yawn, he added, 'By the way, I never did get round ter saying thanks for what tha did that day I had me stupid accident wi' bales. Thaz a grand lad and I'm proud o' tha. And what's more, tha'll mek a grand farmer one day.'

Jamie went to bed after midnight, but tired though he was, sleep evaded him. He was far too excited, running through his mind everything that had happened over the last months, and tried to envision all that was to come. Perhaps he dozed a little. Then, he was aware of light entering his room through the top of his curtains, and he jumped up to pull them back and look out of the window. He saw the dawn rising in the west. A back light brought the shapes of the fells into sharp relief. The blackbird tentatively called and was soon answered by the song thrush.

EPILOGUE

Jamie rode the quad bike over Tinder Fell, with Ben running at his side. They were moving sheep. In front of them, the flock flowed like milky liquid down to the valley; the few that leaked out of formation were quickly rounded up and ushered back by Ben. The gate was already open and once they were all through, Jamie jumped off the bike and shut it. This was one thing a dog couldn't do.

It was mid-August and after a rainy three weeks during which they'd dodged heavy showers to get the grass crop in, the weather now blazed hot. Sally had driven him and Josh into school that morning to get their exam results. Josh was wearing his khaki 'RVK' uniform, and had to go into work afterwards.

Rushing to join his peers in the queue, Jamie had trembled with excitement and dread that was far worse

203

than waiting to hear that he'd passed his tractor driving test, back in June. The order in which the envelopes were distributed was alphabetical of surname, so he and Josh were in the first batch…

His hands had been shaking as he tore it open. He read it three times to be sure and then again. One grade 9, the highest possible mark! This was for design technology. Then he'd got two 8's, four 7's, a 6 and a 5; this was for French, but still a pass. For a few minutes, he'd been involved in the hysterical melee of screaming and high-fiving students. Wilko and The Crawler both warmly congratulated him and mentioned there was still room to join the sixth form. How chuffed he'd felt in telling them that he was going to agricultural college and intended to confirm his place that very afternoon. Glancing around for Moira, he spotted her whooping it up with a crowd of girls. In all the excitement of jumping around and shrieking, she hadn't noticed him and he hesitated before taking a step towards her.

Then, he'd remembered Josh urgently needed to go to work. He'd have to text Moira later. Sally was sitting on a bench near the tennis courts, waiting for him; he'd hurried over to her with a grin, so wide it nearly split his face in two. Josh had also done well, his joy only tainted by the fact that Sophie was still on a month-long holiday in Spain.

As Jamie now reflected on the prom at the end of June, he remembered how he'd felt beforehand, excited, yet nervous and dreading it, a bit like results day. Yet, the prom too, had turned out well. Most of the lads didn't possess lounge suits and had decided to go the whole hog and hire tuxedos. He'd been startled at his transformation when he looked in a mirror and his mum kept saying how handsome he was. She'd wanted to drive him and Josh to the venue. The ultimate of uncool! They'd considered driving there by tractor but Neil advised them of the restricted hotel parking. So the arrangement was that Neil took them and picked them up later. He was dating a girl from Ambleside, so it had suited him.

On arrival, Jamie was daunted by the formality of the elegant lakeside hotel with its terraced gardens, and the fancily dressed people chatting in little groups around the foyer. Then he realised they were all from his past year group. *Creeps! There's the Crawler in a tuxedo and several other teachers to keep an eye on us.* He was nearly knocked out when Sophie appeared at their side, stunning in a tight white satin affair that featured a slit down one side.

Josh whirled her off, and momentarily Jamie stood on his own until Nick Dixon and three other grinning lads sauntered towards him. They laughed together, throwing admiring looks at a little group of girls, until the girls came over to join them. Moira took Jamie's arm and steered him away. She looked beautiful in a long blue dress with her auburn hair cascading down her back. Wow! He couldn't believe his luck and at first blushed like an idiot, whilst his heart jumped for joy. At the end of a wonderful evening, during which they'd talked and danced, she'd moved up close and asked if he'd like to kiss her. Before he could respond, it was she who kissed him, but he wouldn't be telling anyone that, would he?

Riding towards the track that passed the hay barn, he thought about his parents. It was their wedding anniversary today and they'd loved the coffee table he'd made as his exam project. Both had been thrilled with his exam results and the decision he'd taken on his future. They too, had made some decisions over the summer, having applied for a grant to reroof the large barn and a metal building was to be erected to house the cattle. There were also plans afoot for three or four shepherds' huts to rent out as holiday accommodation.

His father was playing music again. No, Martin Bouthwaite hadn't embarrassed his son by joining some oldies' rock band. (That was a relief!) The organist had called in sick at the last minute for a village wedding. Beth had heard about it and somehow she'd persuaded Martin to play. Furthermore, despite protesting, he'd been put on the organists' rota. Jamie laughed to himself as he thought about it. That had been the start. The latest was that a grand piano had just been bequeathed to the village hall from some eccentric old lady's Will, and his father and Sally had already been down to inspect it.

The aroma of barbecue smoke met him as he reached the bottom of the track. Sally had two friends camping near the damson orchard. The Atkinsons were coming over soon. There'd be great food and tunes going well into the evening. In a few weeks he would be at college, where he'd find new challenges and experiences, but for now he'd have a blast with what was left of the summer.

END

ACKNOWLEDGEMENTS

I should first like to thank Helen Haraldsen, whom I originally met many years ago when I took some students to a library related event at her school. As a published author of children's fiction, I came across her again more recently and was inspired to pick up my own writing and aim for publication. Helen mentored me and sent my first draft of Top Thorn Farm to local Young Farmers for feedback. She continues to be a great source of encouragement and advice.

Frances Bowers, another school librarian and learning resources manager, also read my very first draft and printed copies for student feedback. She later read my final version that had undergone many edits, and made a few useful suggestions, for which I'm very grateful. Farming detail in the story has needed to be 'reet' as my fictional characters would agree. And to get it as authentic as possible, I needed to talk to real Cumbrian farmers. So, thanks must go to my friend Helen Woof, who has patiently answered my many questions and explained practices and routines in the farming year.

Thank you to Gemma Sosnowsky, another school librarian, who has given helpful feedback from her student readers.

Huge thanks goes to Amanda at Let's get booked, who has edited Top Thorn Farm and has been so helpful (and patient), with comments and suggestions. I am grateful to her also for the striking cover design and format; I would certainly recommend her services to any aspiring authors.

Finally, I want to mention members of my own family and friends who've put up with me talking about my book over the last few months and given helpful feedback on the cover design. Thank you!

ABOUT THE AUTHOR

Denise holds a BA and MA from Lancaster University, has worked as a secondary school librarian and is a primary school governor.

She loves reading and the wild landscapes of rural Cumbria, where she lives and enjoys long walks with border collies Bess and Flo.

Printed in Great Britain
by Amazon